YEARS OF RED DUST

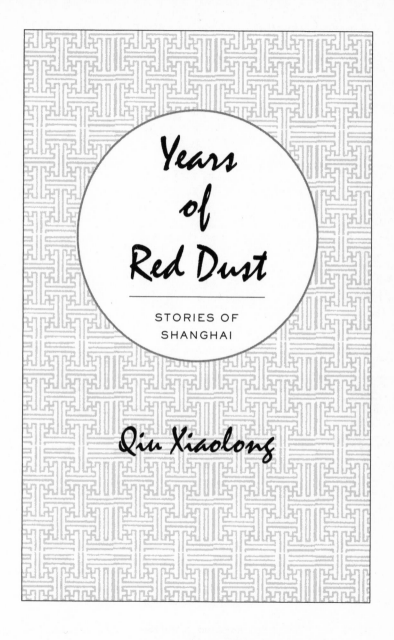

Years of Red Dust

STORIES OF
SHANGHAI

Qiu Xiaolong

ST. MARTIN'S PRESS NEW YORK

This is a work of fiction. All of the characters, organizations, and events portrayed in this novel are either products of the author's imagination or are used fictitiously.

YEARS OF RED DUST. Copyright © 2010 by Qiu Xiaolong. All rights reserved. Printed in the United States of America. For information, address St. Martin's Press, 175 Fifth Avenue, New York, N.Y. 10010.

www.stmartins.com

Designed by Kelly S. Too

ISBN 978-0-312-62809-3

The stories in *Years of Red Dust* originally appeared, in French, in *Le Monde* in 2008.

Slightly different versions of "Welcome to Red Dust Lane," "Cricket Fighting," and "Foot Masseur" originally appeared in English in *Asian Literary Review* 11, spring 2009.

A slightly different version of "Chinese Chess" originally appeared in English in *River Styx*, 81/82.

First Edition: October 2010

10 9 8 7 6 5 4 3 2 1

To the people of Red Dust Lane, which I had the
opportunity to revisit and recapture
in an ARTE TV documentary project in 2009.

ACKNOWLEDGMENTS

I want to thank Laurent Greilsamer and Anne Guerand, whose pushing made it possible for the stories to come out first in serialization in *Le Monde*. I would also like to thank the Chinese University of Hong Kong for the fellowship, which enabled me to do the research for the historical background of the stories. And to thank Keith Kahla, as always, for the fantastic work he has done for the book.

CONTENTS

YEARS OF RED DUST

Welcome to Red Dust Lane

(1949)

*N*ow, as your would-be landlord—to be exact, your second landlord, *nifangdong*—I've lived in this lane for twenty years by the end of 1949. For a new college student not yet familiar with Shanghai, looking for a place characteristic of the city, a place that is convenient, that is decent, and yet inexpensive, Red Dust is the best choice for you. For the real Shanghai life, I mean.

Red Dust Lane—what a fantastic name! According to a feng shui master, there is a lot of profound learning in the choice of a name. No point in selecting insignificant words, but none in pompous words, either. The evil spirit might get envious of something too grand or good. We're all made of dust, which is common yet essential, and the epithet *red* lends a world of difference to it. All of the connotations of the color: human passion, revolution, sacrifice, vanity . . .

You are an honest, hardworking young man, I know,

so I hope you will become one of my subtenants here. Let's take a walk along the lane, so you can really see for yourself.

The first record of the lane is from the late Qing dynasty. Look at this impressive street sign written in the magnificent calligraphy of a Qing dynasty *Juren*—a successful civil service examination candidate at the provincial level. After that, it was developed as part of the French concession, though not as a central part of it. Indeed, so many changes, like the white clouds in the sky—one moment, a gray dog; the next moment, a black weasel . . . Of course, now things are changing again. The Communists are advancing with flying colors and the Nationalists retreating helter-skelter. But the one thing under the sun that will never change, I assure you: this is a most marvelous lane.

Think about the location—at the very center of Shanghai. To the south, the City God Temple Market, no more than fifteen minutes' walk, where you can enjoy an amazing variety of Shanghai snacks. To the north, you can stroll along to Nanjing Road, the street-long shopping center of Shanghai. If you prefer the fancier stores on Huaihai Road, it takes no more than fifteen minutes to get there. On a summer night, you may occasionally smell the characteristic twang from the Huangpu River. Strolling around those foreign buildings lined up along the Bund, like the Hong Kong Bank or the Cathay Hotel, you may feel as if the river were flowing through you, and the heart of the city beating along with you.

Our lane is medium-sized with several sublanes. Another plus, I will say. The front entrance opens onto Jinling Road. There, just a block ahead, you can see the Zhonghui Mansion—the high-rise owned by Big Brother Shen of the notorious Blue Triad, now down and out in Hong Kong. Karma. As for the back entrance of the lane, it leads into the Ninghai Food Market. In case of an unexpected visitor, you can run out in your slippers and come back with a live carp still gasping for air. In addition, there are two side entrances on Fujian Road, with a cluster of small shops and stalls. And peddlers too. Nothing can beat the location here.

This lane, or *longtang*, of Red Dust, may in itself tell you something of Shanghai history. After the Opium War, the city was forced open to the Western powers as a treaty port with areas selected as foreign concessions. The expatriates were then unable to tap the immense potential of the city, so some Chinese were allowed to move in. Soon the concession authorities had collective dwellings built for them in the designated lots. To make them convenient to manage, the houses were designed in the same architectural style, then arranged in lines like barracks, row after row, accessible to the main lane from sublanes. As in other lanes, most of the buildings in Red Dust belong to the *shikumen* style, the typical Shanghai two-storied house with a stone doorframe and a small courtyard. In the early concession days, a *shikumen* house was designed for one family, with rooms for different purposes—wings, hall, front room, dining room, corner room, back room, attic, dark room, and *tingzijian*, a cubicle above the kitchen. As a result of the city housing shortage, some of the rooms were leased. Then individually subleased, with the rooms further partitioned or subdivided, so now a "room" is practically the space for a family. You may have heard of a comedy called *72 Families in a House*, which is about such an overcrowded housing situation. Red Dust is not like that. There are no more than fifteen families in our *shikumen*, you have my word on it.

In Red Dust, people of differing social or financial status are mixed together. Small-business owners or executives take the wing or a floor, while ordinary workers choose the back room or the attic. As for the *tingzijian*, it usually goes to those struggling men of letters—the *tingzijian* writers. They are really fantastic places for creative souls, with constant inspiration coming from the lane.

Indeed, your life is incredibly enriched with all the activity and interaction of the lane. You become part of the lane, and the lane, a part of you. Through the open black-painted door, you see this first-floor hall, don't you? It was turned into a common kitchen area long ago, with the coal stoves of a dozen or more families all squeezed in, along with pots and pans, coal briquettes, and pigeon-house-like cabinets hung on the walls. Squeezed, but not necessarily so bad. Cooking in here, you may learn the recipes of provincial cuisines from your neighbors. Coming back soaked one rainy night, you don't have to worry about catching a cold: a pot of ginger tea is being brewed for you on your neighbor Uncle Zhao's stove, and Elder Sister Wu will add a spoonful of brown sugar into the steaming hot drink. Nor will you find it monotonous scrubbing your clothes on a washboard in the courtyard, where Granny Liu or Auntie Chen will keep you informed of all the latest news of the lane. Some say Shanghainese are born wheelers and dealers. That's not true, but there may be something of that which comes out of the way people in Shanghai have always lived in a kind of miniature society, constantly handling relationships among close neighbors.

People get together a lot not only in the *shikumen*, but in the lane too. Their rooms being so crowded, people need to find space elsewhere. All day long, the lane is vibrant with life—informal, relaxing, and spontaneous. In the early gray light, women will come out in their pajamas, first carrying chamber pots, then later hurrying to the food market, returning with full bamboo baskets and preparing food in the common sinks of the lane while spreading the gossip heard overnight. Men will stretch out, practicing Tai Chi outside, brewing the first pot of Dragon Well tea, singing snatches of Beijing opera, and exchanging a few words about the weather or the political weather. For lunchtime, those people at home will step out again, holding rice bowls, chatting, laughing, or exchanging a slice of fried pork for a nugget of steamed belt fish. In the evening, Red Dust gets

even more exciting—men playing chess or cards or mahjong under the lane lamp, women chatting or knitting or
washing. In summer, it is so hot inside that some will take
out bamboo recliners or mats. And a few even choose to
sleep out in the lane—

Let's take a turn here. Watch out for the droplets from
the laundry on these bamboo poles across the sky of the
lane. An American journalist once said that the colorful
clothing festooned on a network of bamboo poles presents an Impressionist scene. But according to a folk belief,
walking under women's underwear may bring bad luck.
Whether you believe it or not, it can't hurt to take a detour.
And that's another convenience of those sublanes. You can
move through the lane a number of different ways. Here
we are, coming to the front entrance of the lane.

Oh, look at those people gathered here, sitting on bamboo chairs, wooden stools, and holding teas, cigarettes, and
paper fans. This is another special thing about the lane. The
evening talk of Red Dust Lane—Red Dust talk.

You may well find chess and card games and talk among
neighbors in other lanes of the city. But what is going on
here is truly one of a kind. Some people have moved away
but still come back to Red Dust for the evening talk. It is
a time-honored tradition here. Except in bad weather, a
group of people always turns out for the evening conversation of the lane and about the lane.

Now what's special, you may say, about neighbors talking? Well, what makes it unique is the way they make

a story out of everything, a way of seeing the world in a grain of sand. Of course, the lane residents don't invent stories with real heroes or heroines—certainly not the type of "the talented scholar and beautiful girl" or "unrivaled kung fu master." Nor stories with conflicts or climaxes as in books. Still, our storytellers try all kinds of experiments, traditional or avant-garde, flashing back and forth, showing but not telling, sometimes narrating from a special point of view, and sometimes from all points of view.

Since the characters are real people, the evening talk is enhanced through its interaction with the real Red Dust life. While listening to a story, we offer interpretations from our own perspectives, and contributions too, if we happen to know something the narrator knows not. After all, a narrator is not always that reliable, what with their told or untold reasons for making an omission or alteration. The audience knows better and is capable of pulling a story to pieces and retelling it in different ways.

A written story inevitably comes to an end at the last page of a book, whether happily ever after or not. Nothing is like that in real life. You can put an end to your narrative one intoxicated evening, but in a few years, there will be some new development or unexpected twist. A comedy turns into a tragedy, or vice versa, which changes the meaning of the earlier story. Needless to say, sometimes we also play a part, however inadvertent or insignificant, in the stories of others, which, in turn, come to affect ours.

Now look at this young man sitting in the center of the group. He's called Old Root—his surname is Geng, a homonym for "root," and he invented the nickname for himself. According to him, "old" in Chinese does not necessarily refer to one's age; it also connotes wisdom and experience. Though in his twenties, he has an old head on his young shoulders. Self-educated, he reads books like someone swallowing dates without worrying about their pits. Like the proverb goes, the water does not have to run deep: a dragon in it will make it special. Judging from the position of his chair, he must be the storyteller for the evening.

Oh, there's a blackboard leaning against his chair. I don't know anything about the blackboard, but there must be something exciting about it. And sitting next to him is Four-Eyed Liu, another bookworm, who likes to give his newspaper-based interpretation to everything. And Big Hua, who is as curious as a cat. Let's stay here and listen here for a while. Don't worry about the time. If it gets late, I will buy you a night snack—as your second landlord in Red Dust Lane.

Do you remember the opening lines of the *Romance of the Three Kingdoms*? After peace comes war, and after war comes peace. Things are just like that, an endless repetition in this mundane world of ours. Time rolls up and down, waves upon waves, leaving behind, on the moon-bleached beach, stories like shells. Open it, and you may find something after your heart, but if not, don't be too disappointed. It is only a matter of perspective that things appear to be either good or bad. In the year 1949, with the Communists in, and the Nationalists out, there are many things appearing and disappearing, like always, with the change of dynasties.

In the early spring days of 1949, the Nationalist government boasted of making Shanghai an oriental Stalingrad, a turning point in China's civil war, but to the people here it felt unreal. Shortly after Chiang Kai-shek announced his resignation, a monstrous white snake was killed by lightning in Qingpu county—a portentous sign similar to the one at the end of the Qing dynasty. Then panic spread, after news came that the vaults of the Shanghai Bank had been emptied of their stock of bullion. My friend Cai, a waiter in Dexing Restaurant, told me something he saw with his own eyes. For several days in April, the restaurant was reserved by the top commanders of the Nationalist troops. One night, he brought a platter of sea cucumber with shrimp roe to a reserved private room, where he saw a celebrated courtesan reclining naked on the table, feeding her big toe like a fresh scallop to a four-star general, her white foot still flexing to a tune from the gramophone: "After tonight, when will you come back?" Dexing was a genuine Shanghai cuisine restaurant, and these Nationalists knew they could never enjoy a Shanghai banquet again. With high-ranking officials being so decadent and pessimistic, how could the Chiang dynasty not fall?

Well, don't be impatient, my Red Dust fellows. I'm not going to give you a long lecture on the change of dynasties. I'm coming round to the story for the evening, and to the blackboard too. It's just that it always takes one thing to lead to another in this world. Karma in Buddhism, or whatever you want to call it. Things are related and interrelated, though this is not so easily comprehensible to laymen like you or me.

Back to the story. Because of the negative propaganda about the Communists in those days, rich Shanghainese started fleeing the city by whatever means possible—rushing to the airport, to the train station, to the harbor. Like others, in March my boss fled to Taiwan without notice, abandoning the factory. I had to find work to support myself, so I borrowed from the food market a tricycle used for shipping frozen fish bars in its trunk. With the war raging near Ningbo, the market hadn't had a supply of fish for days.

My idea was simple. As people were frantically leaving with all their belongings, transportation within the city had become a huge problem. For some, a tricycle could be the very means they needed, and that presented an opportunity for me. Also, some were getting rid of their things very cheaply. A heavy mahogany Ming-style cabinet of exquisite craftsmanship sold for a silver dollar, I heard. In fact, I myself got a radio for practically nothing. It was the chance of a lifetime—if you had a way to carry what you found.

So I pedaled the tricycle around the swell Upper Corner of the city, venturing into Henshan Road, an area inhabited by fabulously wealthy people with young maids in black dresses, white aprons, and starched caps, and armed guards standing at the gray iron gates. Behind the high walls, those mansions still shone impressively in the afternoon light. It was another reminder of the social polarities—there such a large house was for only one family, while in our neighborhood a far smaller house had to be cut up like pieces of chopped tofu to accommodate a dozen or more families. A red-turbaned Sikh guard hurried over and, ferociously, like an evil-chasing warrior striding out of a superstitious door sign, ordered me to leave. I was suddenly glad at the thought that things were going to change soon.

I decided to try my luck in some less fancy areas, where people also wanted to leave but were without their own cars. I went to Xinle Road, which stretched out silent and nearly deserted almost to the end, where I saw a woman standing alone, in a white raincoat.

She had a couple of purses in one hand and several bags and suitcases heaped on the curb, and she stood in her high-heeled sandals, waving her other hand frantically at any remote resemblance of a taxi—at the moment, the approaching tricycle of mine. As I had guessed, she was anxious to go to the airport. Perhaps in her mid-thirties, she had a willowy figure, fragile against the pile of luggage. There was an elusive quality about her, especially in her large eyes, something that reminded me of a blossoming pear tree, transparent in the late spring. She hesitantly murmured in a distinct Beijing accent that, after purchasing the airline ticket, she did not have much money left. That was possibly true. A ticket those days could have cost a fortune. The tricycle trunk should be enough for all her belongings, among which I noticed a blackboard with the names of Beijing operas written on it.

Then recognition came. She was none other than Xiao Dong, a celebrated Beijing opera actress. I cannot say I'm a Beijing opera fan. Only once could I afford seeing her perform on the stage of the Heavenly Toad Theater. She played Yuhuan, a beautiful Tang imperial concubine, alone in her chamber, drunk, amorous with the fantasy of her lord enjoying rapturous cloud and rain with another imperial concubine. It was such a breathtaking performance, the flowers must have shamefacedly folded themselves before her graceful charm. Xiao was so much more than that. It's hard to put into words. Well, you may have heard those Beijing opera terms—orchid fingers, water sleeves, wasp waist, and lotus blossom steps . . . Suffice it to say that she brought all of them to perfection. You would have to watch her perform to really understand the art of Beijing opera. Many people declared that they were willing to drown in "the autumn waves" of her eyes. I knew better than to have such dreams. Even one of those flower baskets presented to her after her performance cost more than I earned in a whole year.

What's more, she was said to have been pursued by Shen, a business tycoon connected to the Nationalist government as well as the Blue Triad. A couple of years earlier, when she had lost her voice, almost ending her career, Shen helped her, bringing in the best doctor from Germany. After her recovery, he proposed, but she did not consent, because he was a married man. It was not uncommon for such a man to have a second wife or concubine, and her resistance could have ended up like an egg thrown against a stone wall, but to everyone's surprise, instead of using his Triad connections and resorting to force, he kept piling flower baskets against the stage she walked on, smiling and applauding like one under a spell. Then, however, the incredible story of the two was drowned in the headlines of the civil war. I had not heard anything about the pair for a while, and I had no clue how Xiao came to be standing here, all alone.

"You are Xiao!"

"You know me?"

"Why are you leaving Shanghai?" It was none of my business, but I imagined few would enjoy Beijing opera in Taiwan, where most people spoke the Taiwan dialect.

"I have no choice. Shen is dying in Hong Kong." She added, "Sick, broke, his assets all gone because of the war.

He's nobody there, lying in a hospital with needles stuck all over his body. A dragon stranded in a shallow pool is being ridiculed by shrimps."

That sounded like a line from a Beijing opera, the name of which I've forgotten. I was not that thrilled with the quote: though not necessarily a shrimp, I was no dragon in her eyes. Still, her statement overwhelmed me.

Xiao chose not to go to him when he was rich and powerful. Now that he was down and out, she was giving up everything, flying to him at the expense of her career. The city, gloomy with the spreading evening, appeared to be suddenly glistening in her large, lambent eyes.

"Don't worry about the fee. Put as much as you like into the tricycle," I said. "I am your fan."

It was a heavy load, but I pedaled to the airport as if on wings. In the trunk that smelled of the fish she sat, pensive, without her makeup. People could have taken her for someone working for the food market, as her white raincoat, though expensive, looked like a uniform.

At the airport, I attempted to help her check the luggage, but it was hard with so many people trying desperately to get all their belongings aboard. She looked at the blackboard, on which the written characters appeared to have faded, having possibly been worn off by rubbing against the other luggage. She handed the blackboard to me, heaving a deep sigh, in a pose I thought I had seen in a Beijing opera called *Xizi Holding Her Heart*.

"It's the blackboard program for my first day on stage. I

have kept it ever since. You love Beijing opera, I know, so you keep this. I don't think I will ever step on the stage again," she said, as she produced her purse.

I pushed back the money she offered me, my hand touching hers for a split second. "The blackboard more than covers the fee."

Standing outside, I gazed at her retreating figure and listened to the last clicking of her sandals as she disappeared into the somber gate, the sound like a helpless beat made by the night watchman in the Tang dynasty.

My mind was blank until an old proverb occurred to me: a love affair that causes the fall of a city—in a different version, the fall of an empire. In that opera I had seen her perform, Emperor Xuan lost a great empire because of his infatuation with his favorite concubine, Yuhuan. Xiao and Shen reversed the order: it took the fall of Shanghai to finally bring them together.

Humming the tune from the opera, I thought of a Chinese proverb. As a horse proves its strength by galloping a long distance, people get to know each other in times of disaster. And then another proverb came to mind: a beauty's fate is as thin as a piece of paper. I tried to think of some lines of my own, but without success. It's strange that those old sayings function like a retaining wall when the soil begins slipping from the slope.

There's such a lot I do not know about her, I kept telling myself. Why had she not consented earlier, for one thing, if she had cared for him that much? A lot of empty space, but from another perspective, that may be just as well. In a traditional Chinese landscape painting, empty space allows room for imagination. You may laugh at my maudlin sentimentality over a small personal drama during such an important historical time. But in the last analysis, where do we live? In our petty personal lives, not in a history textbook.

I pedaled back home late that night. The sky was occasionally lit up with shells and searchlights. I did not fall asleep at once, instead turning and tossing on the bed. Some time around midnight, the sound of machine-gun fire broke out, seemingly close to the lane. On impulse, I rolled off and crawled under the bed, where I started thinking what I had never thought before, listening to a lone insect chirping at that unlikely hour. After a while, I sneaked out for a look, then came back in to sleep. The night was once again shrouded in silence. I dreamed of a white petrel taking off the runway, soaring over the boundless oceans.

Early in the morning I turned on the radio and heard that Shanghai had been liberated the previous night—the night of May 25, 1949. The Nationalist government collapsed not with a bang, but with an insect's screech. History passed by as I huddled under the bed like a bamboo-leaf-wrapped Zongzi dumpling. The woman announcer on the radio declared proudly, "The city has turned to a new page."

So that is why I'm bringing the blackboard to the evening talk of the lane. Ordinary folks we are, but we must keep ourselves abreast of all the changes happening around us. In this world of ours, things change dramatically as from azure oceans into mulberry fields. So I have a suggestion. Let's start something like a blackboard newsletter. I read about it in a Russian novel—a Soviet novel, I should say—where people post the big events on the blackboard as part of the socialist education. Our people here may not all be able to read newspapers or listen to radios, but from the blackboard newsletters at least we'll have some basic idea of what is happening around us.

This is the last issue of *Red Dust Lane Blackboard Newsletter* for the year 1949. In September, the Chinese People's Political Consultative Conference (CPPCC), exercising the power of the National People's Congress (NPC), adopted the name People's Republic of China for the new state. It is to be a people's democratic dictatorship under the leadership of the working class, based on the alliance of workers and peasants and in unity with all of China's democratic parties and nationalities. It has decided upon Beijing for the country's capital, the five-star red flag for the national flag, and "March of the Volunteers" for the national anthem. On October 1, 1949, on top of the Tiananmen Gate, our great leader, Chairman Mao, declared the founding of the People's Republic of China. Long live the People's Republic of China! Long live

Chairman Mao. The Chinese people are happily bathed in the sunlight of liberation. Here is the new song entitled "The Sky of the Liberated Area Is Bright":

Bright is the sky of the liberated area,
Happy are the people of the liberated area.
The Democratic government loves the people.
Countless are the good deeds of the Communist Party.
Hu hu hu hu hei,
Hu hu hu hu hei . . .

When I Was Conceived

(1952)

This is the last issue of *Red Dust Lane Blackboard News-letter* for the year 1952. It has been another successful year for our young socialist China. In January, Chairman Mao called on the Chinese people to launch a nation-wide campaign against corruption, waste, and bureau-cracy. The Communist Party of China (CPC) Central Committee issued the directive for a campaign against the "Five Evils," with the focus on the owners of private enterprises. Land reform being triumphantly carried out across the country, around 47 million hectares of farm-land owned by landlords have been distributed to 300 million formerly landless peasants. A "study movement of ideological remolding" bore great fruit in educational, intellectual, literary, and art circles. In the ongoing Ko-rean War, the Chinese People's Volunteers won one victory after another. China has raised its international image by signing on to the Geneva War Conventions. At the end of the year, we can say proudly that great progress has been made on the task of restoring the national economy.

It was a dinner that Father and Mother could not put off anymore, having promised early last year, though they were still in no mood for it.

Father, the owner of a hat workshop, had just learned of the necessity of identifying himself as a "capitalist," a word that was crossed out in the new class system formulated by Mao. It might be unwise to invite other capitalists—birds of the same black feather—for a dinner party. Possibly another example of the so-called decadent bourgeois lifestyle. In the year 1952, when young socialist China was said to be surrounded by class enemies, the working-class people of Red Dust Lane watched, on high alert.

Bu Xie, one of their close friends, was leaving for Hong Kong, and they knew why. The campaign of land reform had been in full swing throughout the country, and one of Xie's relatives, a landlord in Zhenghai, had been executed because of his mumbled complaint about turning over the land certificate. What would the campaign of socialist transformation of private enterprises be like in the city? Xie was pessimistic about it, and much of his capital already had been transferred to Hong Kong. Father and Mother wondered when they would ever see him again. Arranging this "seeing-off" dinner party was the least they could do.

In spite of the short notice, Mother had prepared every-thing. The table was an impressive sight. Chopsticks, spoons, and plates lay neatly aligned with folded napkins. The small brass hammer shone among the blue and white saucers. A glass bowl of water stood in the middle.

Father was touched by the sight of her working like a thousand-armed Guanyin in the kitchen, her white short-sleeved shirt molded to her sweating body. It was not an easy job for her to produce such a meal all by herself. Squatting at the foot of a granite sink, Mother was binding a live Yangchen River crab with straw. Several other crabs were crawling noisily on the sesame-covered bottom of a wooden pail.

"You have to bind a crab like this," Mother explained, in response to the puzzled look on his face, "or it will shed its legs in the steamer."

"But why all the sesame on the bottom of the pail?"

"To keep the crabs from losing weight, they have to be provided with enough nutrition before they are cooked. I bought the crabs early in the morning."

"You've really put in a lot of work."

"No need to be so tense all the time, husband. We should have fun tonight."

When she finished concocting the special crab sauce of vinegar, soy sauce, sugar, and ginger slices, their guests started to arrive, one after another.

They, too, immediately fell to talking about the crabs, as if those doomed crawlers were the one and only topic for the day, while Mother hustled and bustled in the kitchen and Father poured out one cup of tea after another. No one mentioned Xie's coming trip to Hong Kong.

On the cloth-covered table, the crabs soon appeared, rounded, red, and white, in golden bamboo steamers. The nicely warmed yellow rice wine shone amber under the soft light. On the windowsill, a glass vase held a bouquet of chrysanthemums perhaps two or three days old, thinner, but still exquisite.

"It's almost like an illustration torn from the *Dream of the Red Chamber*," Bookworm Cheng said.

None of their other guests, Father reflected, seemed interested in the poetic image depicted in the classic novel. Like him, they were oppressed by the unbearable heaviness of being capitalists in the new socialist China, in spite of Mother's effort to cheer them up.

"Remember what Su Dongpo said about crabs?" Xie responded. " 'O that I could have crabs without a wine supervisor sitting beside me.' "

"Don't worry. It's a family meal. There's no wine supervisor here," Mother said, smiling.

Their dialogue failed to spark any response from the other guests. Cheng alone went on. "Remember what Granny Liu says about the crab feast in the *Dream of the Red Chamber*?"

"About the cost of a crab feast—more than half a year's income for a poor farmer?" Zhou, the owner of a small perfume factory, said with a touch of irritation. "How long does the Jia family keep that up in the novel?"

"Eat the crab," Father said, recalling that in the novel, the Jia family soon went to ruin after the crab dinner. "Don't talk about it."

The conversation at the table then drifted in dissimilar directions, among which each and every family had, as it turned out, a difficult script to read.

The Zhous knit their brows into two deep dead knots. In addition to the Party-led union issues in the factory, they faced a crisis at home. Their only son had tried to join the Communist Party by denouncing his parents. An irrevocable breakup, conceivably. "It cannot be helped," Mrs. Zhou sighed, breaking a crab leg.

Mr. Liu's pharmaceutical business was booming because of the Korean War, but still the man worried. He was upset about his third concubine, who was taking a political economy class at an evening school. "She came back in a jeep late last night. In whose jeep—can you imagine?" Mr. Liu continued without waiting for an answer. "The army representative of the city government assigned to my company."

"The People's Liberation Army representative with the red star on his cap?" Shen cut in. "Well, you don't have to worry. The army representative will bring in more business for you. "

"There's no free silver falling from the sky." Liu crushed

a crab shell with his fist instead of the brass hammer. "It's a world turned upside down. Is there ever a cat that will not steal fish?"

Having finished the digestive glands of a female crab, Cheng turned its entrails inside out. They looked like a tiny monk sitting in meditation on his palm. "In the Legend of the White Snake, a meddlesome monk has to hide somewhere after ruining the happiness of a couple. Finally he gets himself into a crab shell. It's useless. Look, there's no escape."

No one appreciated his crab story, which he had told at the wrong place and time. It was a reminder of what they were trying not to think about. Bookworm Cheng took a sip in silent embarrassment while Mother turned on the radio.

"The Chinese People's Volunteers are fighting against the American troops in Korea, in the hardest trench warfare." The woman announcer's voice had a ring of pride. "Our heroic soldiers are overcoming unimaginable hardship, some going without a bite of food for days, and only urine to drink."

From the end of the street came, as if in response, the boom of the drums and gongs celebrating a new national campaign against the Five Evils—bribery, tax evasion, theft of state property, cheating on government contracts, and stealing economic information—all directed against the "black capitalists." A neighborhood committee had been formed recently, focusing on struggle against the class enemies. The neighborhood activists were out celebrating and propagandizing one political campaign after another. Amidst the drums and gongs, they were singing a new song entitled "Socialism Is Good."

Socialism is good, socialism is good.
People enjoy high status in a socialist country.
With the reactionaries knocked down,
The imperialists fled with their tails tucked in.
The people of the whole country are united,
Bringing a high wave of the socialist construction.

Father felt the drums and gongs beating on his heart. So did his guests, perhaps. Father cut his thumb in a crab cracker. An ominous sign. It could be the last crab feast for them. According to a Chinese proverb, the walls have ears. One of their neighbors in the lane—or even one of them in this dining room—could report them to the police bureau or to the neighborhood committee. It would not take much for the Party authorities to conclude that they were capitalists gathering in a conspiracy against the Party.

The Oolong tea leaves floated in Xie's cup, black, untouched. He left abruptly, without staying over for a game of mahjong or doing justice to Mother's dessert—miniature buns with crabmeat stuffing. Other guests followed, making one excuse or another.

Soon Father and Mother were left alone in the silent room, except for several live crabs still crawling cacophonously on the sesame-covered bottom of a wooden pail close to the door.

"Drunk and desolate, they're going to part. / The parting moon sinks in the vast river," Father murmured to himself. They were lines from the poet Bai Juyi, which he had refrained from quoting to Xie.

The table suddenly looked like a battlefield deserted by the Nationalist troops in 1949—broken legs, crushed shells, scarlet and golden ovaries scattered here and there—with confused sounds of struggle and flight into the night. Father suggested that Mother leave the table alone.

They sat on two chairs drawn next to the window. He did not start speaking immediately. She reached out to smooth his jaw and picked a bit of crab from his teeth. He held her hand in his for an extra moment.

The sight of a leaf falling in a swirl outside caught their glance. Silently, they rose and moved upstairs to the bedroom. There was nothing else for them to do, or to say. They had nothing but each other.

They made love, earlier than usual, that night.

In the silence afterward, Father did not fall asleep. There was a faint sound creeping over from a corner near the door. He lay listening nervously for a long while before he remembered that several live crabs remained unsteamed in the wooden pail. Worn out, they were hardly crawling on the sesame-covered bottom of the pail. What he heard was the bubbles of crab froth, bubbles with which they moistened each other in the dark.

Return of POW 1

(1954)

This is the last issue of *Red Dust Lane Blackboard News-letter* for the year 1954. It has been a year full of significant events for the young republic. The First National People's Congress of China adopted the Constitution of the People's Republic of China. Mao Zedong was elected Chairman of the People's Republic of China. In April, a Chinese delegation headed by Premier Zhou Enlai attended the Geneva conference on a peaceful solution to the Korean question and the restoration of peace to Indochina. A new socialist construction project, the Xikang-Tibet Highway linking Yann with Lhasa and the Qinghai-Tibet Highway linking Xining and Lhasa, triumphantly opened to traffic.

The news of Bai Jie's death in the Korean War came to Red Dust Lane in early 1953. A young nurse in the Chinese

People's Volunteers, she was barely twenty that year. According to her comrades-in-arms, Bai was hit by a stray bullet during a disorderly retreat. There was no possibility of recovering her body under the circumstances.

Her picture appeared in the city newspapers. Her noble deeds were lauded on the radios. She was awarded, posthumously, the Second Class Merit Citation. Her family became a Revolutionary Martyr's Family, sporting a red paper flower on their door. Her parents, though inconsolable, shone with tear-glistening pride as a glittering statue was presented to them during a neighborhood meeting. They were invited everywhere to talk about their heroic daughter. More and more people came to learn about her short, glorious life.

When Bai left for the Korean War, she had just finished nursing school and had started working in a hospital. Her former schoolmates remembered her as a bright, hard-working student who got straight A's in every subject, was active in political movements, and was pretty too—her long plaits fluttering on her bosom like soft willow shoots on a spring morning and her cheeks reflecting the peach blossoms in a vernal breeze. She had many secret admirers at school and in the neighborhood too. She was truly like the first dazzling ray of the sunlight that lit up the moss-covered common concrete sink in the lane.

For days, brokenhearted young men appeared in Red Dust Lane. Bai was honored even in the lane's evening talk, with the "Battle Song of the Chinese People's Volunteers"

playing solemnly on the radio, and old and young joining
to observe a minute of silence.

> *In great spirits, with vigorous strides,*
> *We march across the Yalu River!*
> *To protect peace, to defend the land,*
> *It is to guard our home.*
> *Good sons and daughters of China*
> *Are united closely*
> *To resist America, to aid Korea,*
> *And to beat the ambitious US wolves.*

Everybody was bursting with hatred toward the American aggressors. The loss of such a young, beautiful life made
the slogan resonant and meaningful to all of us: "Down
with American imperialism!"

However, Bai came back, to the consternation of the
lane, in the middle of 1954. It was like a bolt out of the clear
blue sky. As it turned out, she had been wounded, captured,
put into a prisoner camp, and finally sent home. There was
something like a shroud cast over her family, over the lane,
and over those who had known her.

No one knew what she had experienced while in the
American prison camp, but in the lane it was whispered that
she was now on the list of "Internal Control." No longer a
revolutionary martyr, but under suspicion from the Party
authorities. After all, anything could have happened to her
in the POW camp. Taiwanese and American secret agents

had been sent there, as was reported in the *People's Daily*, with mind-boggling offers to induce the captured Volunteers to secretly betray the People's Republic. No one could guarantee that she had not been brainwashed or bought off. With the UN embargo weighing down the economy, the Nationalist troops sulking across the Taiwan strait, and the American imperialists patrolling the Korean borders, the Party government had to be suspicious of someone who had spent more than a year in the company of the Americans.

Initially, Bai managed to greet us as before. It did not take long, however, for her to realize that people were trying to avoid her. The neighborhood committee was at a loss about what to do with her. There was no welcome meeting held for her in the lane or at the hospital. The red flower disappeared from her door. Then her smile disappeared too, after the secret police came to visit her. We did not know what they discussed behind her family's closed door.

She changed overnight, like a frost-damaged flower.

Indeed, she put us in an embarrassing situation. People knew she must have suffered in the war, but they did not want to get into trouble by associating with someone who was "politically untrustworthy or suspicious." In the light of Chairman Mao's theory of struggle against enemies everywhere, her unexpected and unexplained return bespoke, to say the least, of political unreliability. And people could not be too careful.

Bai resumed her work at the hospital, but no longer as the head of the political study group there. Nor did she serve in the operating room. The hospital boss was worried about sabotage by class enemies, especially when high-ranking Party cadres were on the operating table. So she was reassigned to cleaning the hospital, working as more of a janitor than anything else. In Mao's discourse, all the changes made no difference so long as the goal was to "serve the people." But people knew there was a difference. Bai might not be classified as a class enemy, nor persecuted or tormented, but she was politically written off.

She was too clever a girl not to be aware of all this, but what could she possibly do, except hang her head low, like one with a sign on her forehead? She no longer talked to her neighbors, instead hurrying in and out of the lane as if she had wrapped herself up in a cocoon.

She was, in fact, literally wrapped up. In the early fifties, people dressed pretty much the same all year round. Still, they would loosen up a little in the lane, in the summer, leaving a couple of buttons undone. Bai, on the contrary, always wore long-sleeved shirts buttoned up to her chin and long pants covering her feet, even on a hot summer day.

This, too, seemed to support a whispered speculation that something had happened to her in the POW camp. People had read and heard graphic stories of what Japanese soldiers had done to Chinese women during the Second World War. The American barbarians could not have been that different.

One evening, Young Hu joined the evening talk, waving a magazine in his hand. "Guess why Bai keeps herself wrapped up all the time?" Hu went on without waiting for a response. "Here's an article about prisoners being raped and branded in Japanese prison camps. There is no question about it now. Branded!"

"You're sick," Old Root snapped. "How can you talk like that? Everyone listen, anyone bringing up the subject again will not share the same sky with me."

A refusal to "share the same sky" was a strongly worded expression. No one had expected such a reaction from Old Root, who was just one of her neighbors, though an avuncular one. After his unexpected interference, the gossip about her unrevealed secret subsided.

At the end of the year, Bai looked like a totally changed woman—like a stuffed scarecrow, gesticulating in the wind, trembling amidst the crows of terror as darkness came falling over the field. It was hard to believe that her beauty could have been shed so quickly, like pear blossom petals after a storm.

"The white petals stamped over and over on the wet, black ground," Old Root commented. "Resurrection is terrible."

(Tofu) Worker Poet Bao I

(1958)

This is the last issue of *Red Dust Lane Blackboard Newsletter* for the year 1958. It has been another victorious year for China in the socialist revolution and socialist construction. In January, the CPC Central Committee convened a conference to discuss the prospects for the Second Five-Year Plan. In April, the first rural people's commune was founded in Henan province. In May, the CPC adopted the general line of "going all out, aiming high, and achieving greater, faster, better, and more economical results to build socialism." Then the CPC Political Bureau decided to double the steel production of the previous year. All these sparked "the Great Leap Forward" movement. Across rural China, 90.4 percent of all households were incorporated into people's communes.

It was in the mid-fifties that Bao Hong moved into Red Dust Lane from Ningbo, where he had been a young apprentice in the local tofu shop. Confident of his tofu-making skill, he had intended to pursue the same profession in Shanghai. In 1958, following Chairman Mao's call for unprecedented development of the steel industry in "the Great Leap Forward," Bao got a job in Shanghai No. 3 Steel Plant instead.

That year witnessed, among other political movements, a nationwide campaign called Red Flag Folk Songs, which was aimed at pushing workers and peasants to the forefront as writers and artists. For Chairman Mao, this was not an impulsive decision. As early as 1942, in a talk at the Yan'an Forum on Literature and Art, he had already set forth his theory that literature and art should serve politics. So it was now a matter of necessity that a large team of worker and peasant writers play a dominant role in the construction of the new socialist China.

On an early spring morning, a senior editor of *Liberation Daily* came to the steel plant. Bao happened to be taking a lunch break, wiping the sweat from his forehead, digging into a bowl of rice with fried tofu. As the white-haired editor explained the purpose of his visit to the steelworker, Bao laughed, shaking his head like a rattle-tambourine. "You're kidding. I've only studied for three years in elementary school. If you want me to make a piece of tofu, no problem—you'll have one as white as jade in no time. But how can I write a poem for your magazine?"

"But I'm looking for a worker poet for our magazine," the editor persisted.

"What can I say?" Bao responded. "Look at this piece of tofu. It tastes like rice glue. What's wrong? The soybean. Indeed, what kind of soybean makes what kind of tofu. And the same with the water, which has produced the dull color of this tofu. The peddler's such a lousy one that I'll never buy from him again. Anyway, what an uneducated worker says will never interest an intellectual like you. No, there's nothing you can do about it."

"Hold on. That's fantastic, Comrade Bao. The soybean and the tofu. That's dialectic. It's brilliant. And the water too. Thank you so much."

"What?" Bao was totally lost.

"I will contact you," the editor said, rising, scribbling several lines in his notebook in a hurry. "I definitely will call you, Worker Master Bao."

A couple of days later, the editor called Bao: there was a short poem on the front page of the *Liberation Daily*.

What kind of soybean makes what kind of tofu.
What kind of water generates what kind of color.
What kind of skill produces what kind of product.
What kind of class speaks what kind of language.

The name of the poet, printed in a larger type, was none other than Bao Hong. There was a short editorial note underneath his name saying, "In his simple and vivid language, the emerging worker poet Bao has eloquently spoken the truth: the class struggle is everywhere in our socialist society. While the class enemies will never change the color of their nature, we, the working-class people, will prove our true selves in whatever we choose to do and say. The first two lines are hidden metaphors in parallel, juxtaposing the images with the following statement. The technique is called *xing* in the *Book of Songs*."

As Bao held the newspaper in his hand, his face turned white as a piece of tofu.

"In our socialist revolution and construction so full of miracles, a piece of tofu can be magical too," one of his fellow workers commented by way of a joke. "A tofu worker poet indeed."

"I'm not a tofu worker," Bao protested, his face suddenly scarlet, as if spread with too much red pepper sauce.

However, it was a huge success, that short poem of his, and it was reprinted in the *People's Daily* and several other newspapers. It became one of the most anthologized poems that year.

Soon, a large number of worker-and-peasant poets appeared, like bamboo shoots after a spring rain. Everywhere people could be heard reading and reciting revolutionary poems singing the praise of the Three Red Flags. A poetry competition was staged in the People's Square in the center of the city, and Bao sat at the rostrum as a judge.

Bao himself came up with a couple of heroic lines:

A shout from our Chinese steelworkers,
And the earth has to tremble three times.

After the poetry competition, the mayor of Shanghai shook hands with him at the Second Shanghai Literature and Art Conference. The radio interviewed him. The magazines covered him. The rush of invitations from companies and schools inundated him.

Bao then became a member of the Chinese Writers' Association, which supported a limited number of "professional writers" by providing them with a salary equivalent to the amount they had made from their previous work units. This program was created in the interest of furthering socialist literature and art, Bao declared proudly in the lane, so that a revolutionary worker like him could concentrate on writing at home instead of having to work from eight to five in the steel plant. Xin, the head of the Writers' Association—as well as a veteran Party writer who had attended the Yan'an Forum Talk in 1942—had personally recommended Bao for membership.

Now Bao wrote full-time in his *tingzijian* room, which had a curtained window above one of the lane's common sinks. While washing in the sink, the housewives in the lane could not help standing on tiptoe and peering in. He was seen reading seriously with a pair of glasses, making notes, thumbing through a large dictionary half the size of the table in his room. He came less and less to our evening talk at the lane entrance. When he did, he began speaking like a man of letters, flashing out new terms like "revolutionary realism" and "revolutionary romanticism," which scintillated like his new silver tooth. Soon there were several other poems in the newspapers. In one poem, he said that "we proletariat cannot be tofu-hearted toward the class enemy," which became an instant catchphrase. Another poem written in angry denouncement of the bourgeois intellectuals made its way into textbooks.

> They're no stinking tofu—
> Stinking not only in smell,
> Rotten in taste too.
> Oh, nothing but poop.

At a subsequent lecture given at a college, Bao met a young student fan of his poems, who then married him. All this happened so fast, so magically, as if with a drop of the chemical coagulant in the soybean liquid, tofu was made.

The lane had hardly registered her first visit when she started cooking in the common kitchen as Mrs. Bao. But such speed was not too surprising that year, when Mao said that one day is equivalent to twenty years in China's socialist revolution and construction. When in Bao's company, she made a point of having a black notebook and a red pen with her. The moment he said something unusual, she would write it down. On several occasions, it was said, she succeeded in turning his random remarks into poems and having them published as the latest masterpieces.

One summer evening, the newlyweds were sitting out in the lane, sharing a large piece of watermelon. Like other wives there, Mrs. Bao was trying to collect the watermelon seeds, which could later be fried as a tasty snack, but Bao stopped her.

"Look at the watermelon," he said, spitting the rind into his palm. "Not sweet at all, so dead pale in color, and look at the watermelon seeds too, so small, so deformed. Such a seed can only grow into such a tiny, pathetic watermelon."

"Look at your face," she said sweetly, by way of a joke. "All your pimples stand out like the watermelon seeds."

It did not take long, however, for her to produce under his name a new poem, which was apparently modeled after the first poem he had composed while still working in the steel plant.

> *What kind of seeds grow what kind of melons.*
> *What kind of vines produce what kind of flowers.*
> *What kind of people do what kind of things.*
> *What kind of classes speak what kind of languages.*

The poem brought even larger credit to Bao. More significantly, in the poem he moved beyond the central image of tofu—an important shift, since his neighbors had doubted Bao's ability to make poetry like tofu. The wife basked in the glory of the husband.

People now supposed that Bao was going to move to a better area as a result of his elevated status. But he didn't, and his wife joked about his fondness for the feng shui of their *tingzijian* room. After all, it was here that Bao had enjoyed his turn of luck. So Bao, as a nationally known worker poet, was assigned an additional room on the second floor in the same *shikumen* house, through a special arrangement, which his wife declared he deserved.

The neighbors started to call him Worker Poet Bao. He answered to it with a prompt smile and with a new song that the radio played during our evening talk. It was entitled "The Working Class Are Strong-Backboned":

We the working class are strong-backboned.
Following Chairman Mao, we march forward,
With the country and the world in our heart,
We do not stop on the road of the revolution.
Self-reliant and working hard,
We do not stop along the road of the construction.
Holding the red flags high, we move on courageously.
We're the locomotive of the new era.

"As in an old Chinese saying, when fortune comes your way, there's no stopping it," Old Root commented.

"Room, wife, and fame—what a metamorphosis through a stroke of fortune!" Four-Eyed Liu joined in. "All because of tofu."

"Tofu or no tofu, there's no pushing away your fortune," Old Root followed with a more profound comment, "but how fortune eventually works out, you never know."

Chinese Chess

(1964)

This is the last issue of *Red Dust Lane Blackboard News-letter* for the year 1964. Having weathered the "three years of natural disasters," China has made new, gigantic progress in the socialist revolution and socialist construction. As Chairman Mao pointed out, over the past fifteen years, literature and art associations and their publications have failed to carry out Party politics, having actually slid to the brink of revisionism in recent years. So it is necessary to talk about class struggle every year, every month, every day. In October, China successfully exploded its first atom bomb, and the Chinese government proposed to convene an international conference to discuss the prohibition and destruction of nuclear weapons. On the international front, Premier Zhou Enlai set forth the basic principles for China's support to the other countries.

In 1964, Lihua failed the college entrance examination.

To be fair to him, his scores were not that bad—they were even slightly higher than the enrollment acceptance level—but he suffered from a disadvantage. In the "class status" column of the college application form, he had to put his father down as a clerk "with historical problems," because the older man had been an activist in a student organization associated with the Nationalist government before 1949. It was a political stain that, though not serious enough to put the old man on the blacklist of the new society, cast a shadow on Lihua's horizon. Melong, another student from Red Dust Lane, entered Shanghai Teachers College with a score actually lower than Lihua's, because of his worker family background. There was a Party policy frequently quoted in the newspapers: *Family background counts, but not absolutely. What counts more is young people's own political performance.* The second sentence was generally regarded, however, as no more than a decorative veneer.

Still, Lihua's parents wanted him to have another try the following year. Or, as an alternative, to start working in a small eatery through the early retirement arrangement of his father, who had worked there for more than twenty years, standing by a concrete sink in a pair of black rubber shoes, washing dishes from morning to evening. Lihua was not eager to get into his father's shoes, which the old man would kick off the first thing when he arrived back home, revealing water-soaked feet as pallid as salted fat pork. So Lihua made a halfhearted attempt to review the test books, not believing that the second time would make any difference. Instead, he started to play Chinese chess in earnest, trying to bury his head like an ostrich in the world of chess—at least for a while.

Spending four or five hours daily at the chessboard, Lihua soon found himself turning into a top player in Red Dust Lane. At a tournament outside the lane, he was "discovered" by Zhu Shujian, a white-haired chess master who had retired from the Shanghai City Chess Team. Zhu saw great potential in Lihua. Though not ready to acknowledge him as a student yet, Zhu started to take him to competitions among the higher-level players. Unexpectedly, Lihua saw a career option far more tempting than his father's, if he could become a member of the Shanghai City Chess Team. The chessboard presented the possibility of a different world to him, one in which he did not have to worry about his family background, so long as he calculated every move on the board, like with a math problem.

On a July morning, Lihua followed Zhu to a cobble-covered street in the old city section, where Wan Liang was going to play against several challengers in a wheellike succession. A member of the Shanghai City Chess team in the fifties and a runner-up in a national tournament several years ago, Wan had suddenly disappeared from the scene a while back. Lihua was thrilled at the prospect of meeting this legendary figure.

The game had been set up in front of a dingy hot-water shop near the end of the street. Normally, such a game would be held inside the shop, where people could smoke, drink, and sometimes eat as well. The decision to have it outside was probably due to Wan's name, which would draw a larger audience. There were five or six thermos bottles lined up along the curb, and the owner of the hot-water shop, a plump man surnamed Han, an enthusiastic amateur chess player, was rubbing his hands, beaming with pride.

Wan Liang was a gaunt, grizzle-haired man with a constant smile revealing his tea-and-cigarette-stained teeth. He straddled one end of a wooden bench, while his opponent perched on the other end and the chessboard sat between them. There was a tall, worn bamboo broom leaning against the wall behind Wan like an exclamation mark. Stripped to the waist in his black homespun shorts and wooden slippers, Wan appeared sallow, malnourished, his ribs visible like a board in the glaring daylight. They looked like frets on a stringed instrument, and they reminded Lihua of a Shanghai expression: it's possible to play the pipa on his ribs.

Wan was unquestionably a master of the chessboard, but his manner was surprising. He kept lifting one bare foot, and then another, onto the bench. Clasping the yellow sole of his foot in one hand, he held a huge sticky rice ball in the other, unaware of the grain stuck on his nose tip.

What's more, Wan applauded his own moves and criticized his opponent's loudly. With the audience talking, cursing, laughing alongside, Wan seemed to build ever-increasing momentum on the chessboard, peppering the game with sarcastic remarks, making it hard for his opponent to concentrate.

"My horse, it is really galloping in the skies, but the stinking positioning of your soldier really reeks like a dog shit," Wan said, busy nodding or munching at his rice ball. "The way you move your piece—exactly the way a blind man rides a blind horse along a steep cliff on a dark, stormy night. Your head must have been stuffed with straw."

Lihua was growing more and more uncomfortable. After years, if he had the potential and studied hard, he might be able to play a masterful hand like Wan—maybe even as a member of the City Chess Team. But then what?

Wan was like a down-and-out Don Quixote, an old man stripped of his shining armor, holding a broken lance, fighting one absurd battle after another with imagined dignity. Still, Wan was a powerful player, and his tactics, which were not aboveboard, also helped. His tactics of distraction brought unbearable pressure on his opponent, who was befuddled into making one blunder after another. The third game that morning was finished in less than ten minutes.

Lihua didn't know exactly how the challenge matches were arranged. It appeared that each of the challengers had the opportunity to play one or two games with Wan, while at the other end of the bench a line of new challengers waited. Soon, however, there was only one left, a sturdy middle-aged man surnamed Pan, with a bald head, bushy eyebrows, and a determined expression in his beady eyes. Pan played slowly, stubbornly, thinking long and hard before making a single move, in a sharp contrast to Wan's carefree style. Wan started to show his impatience through a variety of new gestures—tapping his fingers at the edge of the board, breathing audibly into the cup, turning to examine the clock inside the hot-water shop . . .

As Pan was holding a cannon piece in the air, debating with himself for several minutes about where to fire, Wan commented with a sardonic smile, "Charge forward, Amier." It was a witty reference to the movie *The Visitor from the Ice Mountains* and the character Amier, a young naïve man too shy to express his love. The audience burst out laughing. Pan's face went scarlet, and he put the cannon down in a surprising position, making a fatal threat to Wan.

Abruptly Wan stood up and left, carrying the bamboo broom, uttering a fragmented sentence—"Got to go"— and hurrying across the street.

No one seemed to be puzzled by this except Lihua. It was not polite, to say the least, for Wan to leave in the middle of the game. Was it possible that he, too, had to think long and hard about his countermove in this critical situation? Could it have been a face-saving trick?

Wan came back in about twenty minutes, throwing down the bamboo broom like a broken lance and, as if without thinking, pushing his castle to the bottom line.

It was a brilliant counterstroke, immediately turning the table. Pan perspired profusely, his face flushing and his fingers trembling.

"What's that?" Wan said, sniffing vigorously. "It smells like a fermented winter melon."

Lihua did not smell anything. Looking around, he noticed one of the onlookers holding a bowl of watery rice in his hand, but he did not see any fermented winter melon in the bowl. "Winter melon?" he mumbled, recalling that it was something like a special pickle for Ningbonese, but the others broke out in guffaws. Lihua realized it was another insulting remark in reference to Pan's skill.

That proved to be the last straw for Pan. "What are you, Wan? Don't forget your class status as a Bad Element! An enemy to the socialist society, you can only sweep the lane like a dog with its tail tucked in. How dare you still be so cocky after two years in prison?"

Wan turned pale, trembling like a leaf torn from the tree.

"Come on, Pan," Zhu intervened. "A game is just a game. Don't talk like that."

"Pee and see if the reflection of your own stinking ass is clean. You played chess for a warlord before the liberation in 1949," Pan snapped, with a couple of blood vessels on his temples standing out, wriggling like nightcrawlers. "You think we revolutionary people don't know that? It's the age of the proletarian dictatorship."

Zhu was speechless with rage. Han, the owner of the

hot-water shop, came over to Pan, holding a cup of fresh, hot tea. "Give me face, Pan. After all, the game is in front of my shop."

"What face do you have? A face of a small-business owner! Your own class status is just one shade less black than Wan's. Mind your damned hot-water business!"

"You're biting like a mad dog today. Have I ever charged you for the tea you've drunk for so many years? Even a dog knows how to shake its tail in appreciation." Han was furious as well, dashing the cup against the concrete curb. "What's wrong with my class status? My son is a PLA soldier!"

Pan was beside himself, throwing the chessboard to the ground with a forcible sweep of his arm. All the pieces rolled about like soldiers falling downhill in the disastrous retreat of the Qin army in the ancient Feishui battle . . .

Lihua did not see how the fiasco ended, and he left alone, in no mood to reexamine the chess game, step by step, as he usually did.

That night, he decided not to take the college entrance test again, and he took over his father's job, washing dishes in the small eatery.

Shoes of the Cultural Revolution

(1966)

This is the last issue of *Red Dust Lane Blackboard Newsletter* for the year 1966. In this year, our supreme leader Chairman Mao launched forth the Great Proletarian Cultural Revolution to seize back the power from the revisionists in the Party, like Liu Shaoqi and Deng Xiaoping. The Central Cultural Revolution Group, directly under Mao, took over control of *People's Daily* and published an editorial entitled "Sweep away All Monsters." Mao wrote to the Red Guards, the new student organizations all over the country, supporting their rebellion against the reactionaries. On eight occasions, at Tiananmen Square, Mao reviewed Red Guards, groups whose number has now reached more than thirteen million. In response, Red Guards have relentlessly subjected the class enemies to mass-criticism and crushed the old establishments. In the midst of the slogans of the Cultural Revolution, China tested its first guided missile carrying a nuclear warhead.

The Cultural Revolution hung
a halter of ragged shoes
around her neck: heels,
mules, slings, boots, sandals,
her bare feet bleeding . . .

"Why those ragged shoes?" a boy asked his grandfather in the midst of the spectators that lined the lane like tree ear fungi.

"Symbolic," his grandfather said. "Heaven alone knows how many men might have had her."

"Like those dirty shoes," his father said, "she must have been worn out by such a number of them. She was a famous actress before 1949!"

"But that was almost twenty years ago," the boy said.

"Twenty years ago," his uncle cut in, "you could not have touched her little toes for thousands of yuan. Today, I have placed a wreath of shoes around her neck."

"So those are your own shoes." The boy nodded in enlightenment, staring at people's spittle shining on her face and at the red line of footprints drying behind her.

Her mad song to the ragged shoes:

Shoes, shoes, shoes, shoes
of the Cultural Revolution;
shoo, shoo, shoo, shoo,
barefoot is the solution.

Cricket Fighting

(1969)

This is the last issue of *Red Dust Lane Blackboard News-letter* for the year 1969. In this year, our Party and people have achieved great victories in the course of the Cultural Revolution. In the Ninth CPC National Congress held under the presidency of Chairman Mao, Lin Biao, Mao's close comrade-in-arms and successor, delivered the political report confirming the theory and practice of the Cultural Revolution. A new Political Bureau was formed. China successfully conducted its first underground nuclear test.

In the summer of 1969, evenings began hilariously with cricket fighting in a corner close to the end of Red Dust Lane, where people brought out their clay cricket pots, squatted in a circle, and watched their crickets fight against one another. After a fierce battle, the winning cricket would sing loudly by scratching its wings in the pot, while the defeated would run for its life, circling the pot or jumping out. The cricket owners and onlookers would join in by shouting or shooing, as if the fate of the whole world depended on the outcome in the small pot.

As an elementary school student, I was glued to the corner, though too young to own a cricket. There was no possibility my parents would allow me to go cricket catching in the countryside. In the days before the Cultural Revolution, some people had gambled on cricket fighting, and my parents did not like the association. But they acquiesced to my watching the nightly fights, as long as it kept me in the lane.

One evening that summer, Cousin Min gave me a cricket he had caught in a graveyard in Qingpu. It was nicknamed Big General, and it was not exactly big but it was pitch black, with one third of its head made of two gigantic teeth, glaring like a pair of axes in the sun. At the time, people believed in the spirit of the earth, and whatever grew up in the graveyard, they declared, must have acquired its yin spirit. So it was a hell of a cricket, and I wondered why Min wanted to give it to me.

"There is no time," he said simply. "We have to fight for Chairman Mao."

It was the fourth year of the Cultural Revolution. With the old government system demolished, Red Guard organizations found themselves in power, and then they found their interests in conflict. Each faction claimed to be the most loyal to Chairman Mao and denounced the other as the most treacherous. Fights among different organizations broke out, initially with words, then with stones or knives, and finally with guns.

I understood so little of it. Nor did I care. It was the first time that I owned a cricket. Oh, what a grown-up's prestige came with such a valuable possession! In the corner, people talked to me like an equal, even going out of their way to be nice, especially when they wanted Big General to fight their crickets. I learned such a lot about cricket fighting, like how to choose the feed, how to make a temporary bamboo container, how to improve the housing, how to trim a cricket-goading rush stem, and how to keep the pot warm in cold weather.

Of course, what really made it a brave new world for me in the lane was the Big General. Having absorbed the infernal spirit of the graveyard, the cricket attacked its opponents like hell—leg-ripping, jaw-cutting, and belly-slitting—in the purple arena of the clay pot. The first day I put it in to fight in the pot, it defeated five crickets in a row, breaking the record of Red Dust Lane.

It kept winning enthusiastic applause for itself, and for me. Beneath its left wing, there was a tiny orange dot shaped much like the mole on Mao's chin, though I knew better than to mention it to others. A cricket, I thought to myself, could be the most inscrutable creature in the world, behaving as if born for the purpose of fighting against another—and for its master, I added. I gave it a longer nickname: Invincible Big General Li Yuanba, the number one hero in the *Romance of the Sui and Tang Dynasties*—small, swarthy, wielding two axes like gigantic mountains. Once, when enraged, Li Yuanba tore a mighty opponent into two, thus making a great contribution to the Tang empire. My Big General would do exactly that for me.

Soon, having conquered all its rivals in Red Dust Lane, it began to draw challenges from other well-known crickets outside the neighborhood. Big General's name began spreading far and wide. One of the celebrated veteran cricket fighters came all the way from Yangpu district to take a look at the cricket.

I was eager to report all these victories to Min, of course. I went to his home, but Aunt Xiuxiu told me that Min had to stay in the school. The headquarters of his Red Guard organization, Revolution Thunderstorm, was faced with an armed attack by a rival Red Guard organization, Dispelling Tigers and Leopards, which enjoyed support from a local rebel police organization. So I asked Aunt Xiuxiu to tell Min that the Big General was doing great.

The day after my visit to Min's home, however, the Big General lost a battle to an unknown cricket jumping out of a cheap bamboo container, which, unlike a clay pot, was used only for a second- or third-class cricket. It was utterly inexplicable.

A Chinese proverb says, it's common for a general to win and to lose. Most crickets could resume fighting in a couple of hours, but that was not the case with mine. No matter how I tried to stimulate it with the golden rush stem, it would not throw itself into a fight again. In the pot, to my shamed surprise, it would simply walk away from any approaching opponent, without so much as showing its teeth. If cornered, it jumped out of the pot like a miserable coward.

Soon Big General was booed by all the cricket fighters, and I found myself turning back into an insignificant kid. Fewer and fewer grown-ups in the lane talked to me anymore. In desperation, I consulted with a cricket guru, who gave me several suggestions.

Following his suggestions, I tried to starve the cricket first. The rationale was simple. When hungry, one would fight for food—anything edible or imaginably so. Cannibalism applies to crickets too. It did not work, though. The moment I put the Big General into an opponent's pot, it started feeding itself on the remaining rice like a beggar before fleeing for life. I then tried the pepper-diet experiment. Red pepper was supposed to make its teeth sharp and make the cricket burn to sink them into its enemy. It didn't help, either. Finally, I resorted to the "resurrection" technique. I drowned the cricket in a bowl of water and pulled it out to dry up in the sun until it gradually came back to life. I repeated the drowning and resurrecting process several times. This desperate treatment was supposed to wash the defeatist memory out of its brain, like the River Styx. At one point, I let the cricket stay under the water a bit too long. When I pulled it up, its belly appeared swollen. Still, the Big General managed to come back to life.

While I was bent over at the corner of Red Dust Lane, Aunt Xiuxiu came looking for me. She was worried about Min. His school was surrounded by the Dispelling Tigers and Leopards, with the telephone line cut. Min was still holding out in the headquarters with several loyal comrades, but she had had no news of him for several days. I tried my best to comfort her before I hurried to the cricket fight scheduled that afternoon.

After I repeated the resurrection one more time, the Big General still showed no spirit to fight. In desperation, I tossed it up high into the air. It was a shock technique similar to the resurrection technique: according to my cricket guru, it could concuss a cowardly head into a hellish helmet. To my astonishment, the Big General jumped wildly out of the pot again. In a hurry to grab and recover it, my finger cut off a tiny piece of its leg.

"Great, he's really mad now," my guru observed.

Sure enough, the Big General started to pounce on its opponent as if charging at it from another world. It snapped off half the head of its foe in the first round. It tore off a leg from another. It cut the third fighter's jaw in the same pot. Applause rose from all around, but I began to worry. The Big General was at a disadvantage. Days of starvation, pepper-diet, and resurrection treatments all seemed to be taking a toll. When engaged with Black Devil, the fifth opponent in a row, Big General wobbled on its legs. One of its broken legs might have been bleeding all this time, though it was invisible in the pot. Limping, it hung on doggedly.

I was at the point of quitting on its behalf, but that was against the rules. With their teeth entangled, the Black Devil threw the Big General to its back. Before my cricket recovered its feet, the Black Devil sunk its teeth into its belly. Twitching, the Big General opened and closed its teeth in a valiant effort before it breathed its last breath.

An empty pot in my hand, alone in the corner, I wept when I saw a tiny black spot limping in the sinking sun that evening.

A couple of hours later, I learned that Min had been killed in an attack launched by the Dispelling Tigers and Leopards. He was the last to fall, fighting to the end with a steel cleaver. Disemboweled, he died still clutching a red, shining *Quotations of Chairman Mao* in his mutilated hand.

When President Nixon First Visited China

(1972)

This is the last issue of *Red Dust Lane Blackboard News-letter* for the year 1972. It has been another year full of great victories during the Cultural Revolution. In February, United States President Nixon visited China. He met with Chairman Mao and Premier Zhou. China and the United States issued the Shanghai Communiqué, declaring that there is but one China and that Taiwan is part of China. In September, Japanese Prime Minister Kakuei Tanaka also visited China. The Chinese and Japanese governments released a joint statement declaring the establishment of diplomatic relations between the two countries. We now have friends all over the world.

Nineteen seventy-two started with some major political events hardly comprehensible to Red Dust Lane, particularly to elementary school students like us. Among them was the visit and welcoming of the American President Richard Nixon. In our school textbooks, we had never learned anything positive about American imperialists—they were always the number one enemy to China. How did this change overnight? We asked our parents, who turned out to be just as confounded. Indeed, many things that had happened during the Cultural Revolution were beyond their comprehension.

During the previous year, we had heard of the "stinking-for-thousands-of-years" death of Vice Chairman Lin Biao, Chairman Mao's hand-picked successor, who perished and was condemned as "a heap of dog poop" after an unsuccessful coup attempt. Lin was said to have been against the visit of the American president. Then early this year, Confucius, having been dead for more than two thousand years, was dragged out of the grave as a target for revolutionary mass-criticism. Confucius too had been against foreign barbarians. We figured that all this might have something to do with the change in attitude about Americans.

The neighborhood committee believed it necessary to explain the historical and political significance of the visit to the lane residents. After a two-hour meeting, we remained lost in clouds and mists as before. However, understanding or not, we had to follow any strategic decision made by our great leader Chairman Mao.

Red Dust Lane was listed as one of the highest alert areas during the visit of President Nixon, since it was possible he would pass by here on his way to the Bund or to the City God Temple Market. Security measures had been studied and restudied by the city government.

First of all, each and every potential troublemaker was to be removed. To keep the most vigilant watch over the class enemies, or the "five black classes of people"—landlords, rich peasants, counterrevolutionaries, bad elements, and rightists—as well as the capitalists, the neighborhood committee put them together like straw-bound crabs in the back room of the neighborhood committee office. They were not allowed out of sight for one single minute until the official dismissal notice was given. Of course, that measure alone was by no means enough. At such a crucial juncture of the Cultural Revolution, many could turn into agents for the KGB or CIA, intent on sabotage. Comrade Jun and Comrade Yin, two full-time Party cadres of the committee, would patrol the lane like a couple of wound-up toy soldiers, watching out for any suspicious strangers skulking in or out of the lane. The lane was further divided into four sections, each of which was supervised by a part-time committee member, with Old Hunchback Fang guarding the main lane entrance like Zhongkui, the fierce spirit portrayed as jumping out of the traditional door sign.

But the political responsibilities confronting the lane could be far more complicated. For one thing, troublemakers were not necessarily limited to the class enemies. Curious, people could surge out like human waves looking to get a glimpse of the Americans—which was potentially a diplomatic disaster, interpretable as a sign of China's intense interest in the West. It would be a serious loss of face, to put it in the common language. So the lane residents were ordered not to leave the lane during the day unless it was approved by the neighborhood committee.

President Nixon was supposed to see a clean, beautiful, prosperous city of Shanghai—"in the normal way." Which did not mean that things were to be left as they were, needless to say. Some things were to be left alone, and some were not. For instance, the beggars on the streets had to be made invisible. So would be the dripping clothes on the bamboo poles outside the *shikumen* houses, as well as the peeling big-character posters on the walls and the spiraling smoke from the woks. In addition, the district government demanded that runny-nosed kids, who could unexpectedly run into traffic, be kept off the streets as well.

In short, the order of the day was to follow the Party authorities' instruction to the letter: "China should show the best of the proletarian during the first American president's visit."

To ensure the visit's success, the district government assigned Commissar Liu as a mobile coordinator for several adjoining neighborhoods, including Red Dust Lane. Newly discharged from the army, where he was a reconnaissance platoon head along the China-Vietnam border, Liu appeared to be the most qualified man for the job. Starting at nine o'clock on the morning of the visit, Liu would come equipped with a walkie-talkie and a shining red armband, patrolling every lane and sublane in the area, checking with security people stationed here and there, and passing the latest information around. He was responsible for coordinating with the metropolitan police force and the city authorities and for keeping the neighborhood committees informed of progress during the day or of any change in the schedule. By three o'clock in the afternoon, when the Americans would have returned to the hotel, Liu would come over to announce the lifting of the high security alert.

Still, all this would not have had too much of an impact on us but for a suggestion made by Commissar Liu. He argued that not only preschool kids but also grade school students like us could unexpectedly lead to problematic situations. Schoolteachers might not successfully keep those Little Red Guard students quiet and still in the classrooms. So an urgent notice was given to parents that they were responsible for their children under the age of ten and must either stay with them at home or put them under the collective surveillance of the neighborhood committee. Consequently, a group of the kids from Sublane 3, including me, were gathered together at Lulu's home under the supervision of her grandmother. A decision made on the grounds that her son was a Party cadre.

But Lulu's place was not large. A room of fifteen square meters, with three beds squeezed in for the three generations that lived under the same roof, along with the furniture and odds and ends. For the day, there were nine of us packed in there like sardines. I noticed a transistor radio on the nightstand, but Granny was under special orders not to make any noise. So Qiang and I started a game of army chess on a slip of floor between two of the beds. Lulu made an exquisite red paper cutout of the Chinese character of loyalty, and she danced with the character held high, in front of the portrait of Chairman Mao. Intent on showing her loyalty, she jumped up, missed her footing, and stamped the chess pieces under her feet. Granny suggested that we read our textbooks instead, without knowing that our one and only textbook was *Quotations of Chairman Mao*, most of which we had memorized. I recited to her an appropriate quote for the occasion: "Be determined and not afraid of any sacrifice. Overcome all the difficulties and win the victory."

The victory in question would come around three o'clock, we calculated. Long before noon, however, time started to weigh heavily on us, like the blackboards hung around the necks of the class enemies. For lunch, each of us had a steamed white-flour bun with minced pork and vegetable stuffing, as a delicious incentive from the neighborhood committee. But it did not change the fact that we were stuck for so long in a small, stuffy room with the windows closed. Pig Head Jin started coughing, pressing a fist against his mouth. Little Monkey Xu suffered from bad hiccups. To cover up the unwelcome chorus, Granny sealed the windows with tape and drew the curtain too, which made the room even more like a steamer.

In the semidarkness, the curtain hung motionless like a movie screen, upon which we began to project our imagined images of the outside world. Not far from the lane, Yan'an Road would be becoming a hustle bustle as a part of the anticipated route. Some people would be stationed there, probably not a lot, but at least as many as in a normal day. It would not do for the Americans to see a deserted street. The people chosen would be wearing their spic-and-span Mao jackets, as would the plainclothes cops stationed at each and every corner. Pig Head Jin and I started arguing about one particular detail. He declared that he had once seen a Red Flag limousine during the Romanian president's visit to China. The limousine was made of special bulletproof steel, shining like a black dragon in the sun. Jin thought the American president must be riding around in the same limousine. I differed, saying that the American president and Chinese premier must have come in a convertible, waving their hands to the Chinese people, so that the American people could see it on their TVs across the ocean. TV was said to be something common in the United States, even though there was not a single TV set in our lane yet. We could only stay in the room like caged cats, curiosity-crazed.

Liming then fell to studying the water stains up on the ceiling. The stains appeared to be miraculously connected into dotted lines, merging into a contour of the Rocky Mountains, he maintained in earnest, having recently caught a glance of the mountains in an old textbook map at a recycling center. Qiao, a freckled girl from next door, busied herself hiding-and-seeking among a sweep of drying socks, which Granny had to air inside the room for the day. Qiao developed a Dacron allergy, and she began rubbing her eyes and nose as if suddenly lost to a world of unfriendly, American pollen. (I have heard that she was dumped, years later, because of her incessant sneezing, which caused her then ex-lover to suffer severe insomnia.) As for me, I imagined myself in an airplane on a successful espionage mission unreported in the official newspapers. But my paper airplane knocked itself down against the bare wall of Lulu's room.

What made things even worse was an inconvenience totally unanticipated. There was not a single private bathroom in the lane, as was the case with many other neighborhoods, so at home, people used chamber pots, or went out of the lane to a public bathroom, which was now totally out of the question. In Lulu's place, there was a small cabinet partition made for this purpose, but I found it too hard to excuse myself while in a room packed with several girls my age.

Finally, it was almost two in the afternoon. Granny mumbled to herself. Commissar Liu would soon come to the lane, briefing the neighborhood committee on the status of the tour. If the Americans had passed by, the security alert would be reduced to a less intense level. She stretched her neck out of the window, only to see Old Hunchback Fang crouched at the lane entrance, motionless, more like a disabled cat in the distance.

Granny began to be worried. She had heard a story told by Pony Ba about the assassination of another American president. How true the story was, we did not know. Pony Ba's father was a Bad Element—and was locked in together with other class enemies in the neighborhood committee office at this very moment—who had gotten into trouble for listening to the Voice of America. The tension was building up in the room, and now in the lane too. Soon the uncertainty grew to be almost unbearable.

Still, not a chicken was flying, nor a baby crying, nor a cat jumping. Red Dust Lane held its breath, as if awaiting resurrection. Some wondered whether Commissar Liu could have lost his way, but others brushed aside the possibility. Commissar Liu was a reliable, experienced Party cadre.

As the old clock's hand moved to three thirty, Granny became panicky. Something must have happened. Lulu turned on the radio. No special news. Normally, news about a distinguished foreign guest's visit to the city would not be broadcast until seven o'clock in the evening. She volunteered to go to the neighborhood committee for the latest information, but Granny could not let her go. Every move had to wait until Commissar Liu's arrival, though according to the schedule, the whole thing should have been finished half an hour ago.

Granny was no longer able to contain her anxieties. She had another responsibility: to cook dinner for the family. A punctual soul, she had to start preparing around four, or her day would be totally derailed. She was also seized with an asthma attack, possibly induced by the deteriorating air quality in the room or by her frustration over the impossible dinner. Her lips livid, she desperately needed to breathe fresh air, but her political responsibility demanded she stay shut up in the room. To our surprise, she produced a clay Buddha image hidden in the closet, and she started hugging the image in earnest: *Come back, Commissar Liu, oh Buddha, please allow us to cook, to cough, and to cope.*

Miles away from Red Dust Lane, Commissar Liu did not hear any of those desperate messages. At that moment, he was catching a glimpse of a waitress becoming a legend in Green Waves, a restaurant located by the nine-turn bridge in the City God Temple Market.

Earlier in the afternoon, the Americans had come to the restaurant, which was celebrated for its Shanghai-style delicacies. President Nixon had been very satisfied, offering to shake hands with a young waitress who served at the table and describing her as "delicious" while still smacking his lips over a mini pork-and-crab-stuffed soup bun. The interpreter did an excellent job in translating the compliment. Such an epithet was a revelation, like a magic wand waving in a foreign fairy tale, shining over the waitress in her transparent crystallike plastic sandals. Several reporters rushed over to the one and only pay phone in the restaurant to share the latest news, which then spread quickly, especially among those security personnel with mobile communication equipment, with details being added or modified in quick succession. In one version, President Nixon forgot to bite into the soup bun at the sight of her. In another variation, he bit, but so forcibly that the soup spilled out, and his wife scowled beside him. In every version, the waitress was a graceful beauty beyond description.

The moment the American president left the restaurant, people rushed over from all directions. The waitress was standing behind a large window, cutting crisp-skinned roast pork on a huge stump with a sharp knife. She looked flushed—possibly with the American's praise, though unaware of its instant rippling effect throughout the city. People immediately had excuses for being at her window—to buy some cooked food to bring home after a day's hard work. A queue soon formed outside the window, looking through the glass at this "delicious" girl. Commissar Liu arrived in a great hurry, but he still had to stand at the end of a long line, waiting for an hour before his turn to come to the window. The sun radiated patience in the afternoon as the line inched forward. A fungus appeared out of a wall cranny close to his left foot. Finally, he moved up to the small opening in the window. She was now cutting a Beijing roast duck with its fat still dripping from the stitched ass. An iridescent-eyed fly sucked the sticky duck sauce on her bare rounded toe, delicious as the scallop buns in the banquet in honor of the American president.

A fire hydrant squatting outside the restaurant stared through the glass in outrage. The red armband crumbled in his pocket, Commissar Liu forgot us.

We did not hear anything about the visit that afternoon, nor did we hear in the early evening. In fact, the notice about the return of the American president to the hotel did not come until after nine o'clock that night, when the neighborhood committee called the district government. The details of the incident did not come out until much later, when Comrade Liu (having lost the Commissar title due to his "unforgivable negligence in a political assignment") was allowed to marry the waitress (no longer a "city goddess" once news arrived of the Watergate scandal) after the Cultural Revolution.

By that time, I had started studying aviation science in college.

Pill and Picture

(1976)

This is the last issue of *Red Dust Lane Blackboard Newsletter* for the year 1976. It was a year full of significant events for China. In January, Premier Zhou Enlai passed away, and more than a million people lined the main streets of the capital to express grief and pay tribute to him. At Chairman Mao's suggestion, Hua Guofeng served as the acting premier. In April, people's mourning of the beloved premier at Tiananmen Square was condemned as a "counter-revolutionary incident" and suppressed by force. Deng Xiaoping was removed from all his posts inside and outside the Party. In July, Zhu De, Chairman of NPC, died at the age of eighty-nine. The city of Tangshan was struck by an earthquake measuring 7.8 on the Richter scale, and more than 242,000 people were killed. In September, our great leader Mao Zedong, Chairman of CPC, also passed away. In October, the Party authorities took decisive measures, detaining the Gang of Four headed by Madam

Mao. The CPC Central Committee appointed Hua Guofeng chairman of CPC Central Committee and Central Military Commission. China has finally turned over the page after ten years of the Cultural Revolution.

On a summer afternoon in 1976, Peng Guoqiang had a long, drawn-out discussion with a group of his fellow Red Guards about a poem he had written in praise of Chairman Mao, but what he really was trying to achieve was to impress Jianyin, a pretty girl in the group. During those years, it was out of the question for young people to talk to each other (except about Mao and the Cultural Revolution), let alone date.

The poem was a difficult one. Peng worked hard on the refrain, "a long life to Chairman Mao, a long, long life," trying to rhyme "life" with "strife" and "rife," but someone in the group objected, saying that the rhyming words did not appear proper—that they did not carry enough thematic respect for the organic tone of the poem. It was a tough question. To Peng's surprise, Jianyin supported his effort, saying that the rhyming words did not have to carry reverential meaning in themselves. Her statement was like a cart of charcoal sent in the winter. Afterward, even more to his surprise, as she left the classroom, a small picture of hers fell out of her purse, a picture of a spirited Red Guard with her armband shining in the sunlight and a gold badge of Mao radiating on her youthful bosom. As he picked it up, he wondered whether it was a coincidence but decided not to bother with the question—at least, not while he tried to decide whether or not to return it to her.

Instead of going back home to Red Dust Lane, he went to Bund Park by himself, sitting at a small café there, working and reworking the poem, smoking, stirring the black coffee with a spoon of "political correctness." It was a hard job. He cudgeled his brains out searching for some other words to rhyme with "life," thinking of Jianyin's smile flashing in the sunlight. After he had downed three cups of coffee in quick succession, he was seized with an impulse to rhyme "life" with "die" and "expire," as if possessed. The blasphemous counterrevolutionary lines kept rushing, irrepressibly, onto the tip of his tongue. Sweating all over, trembling like a fallen leaf in the wind, he nearly suffocated himself by stuffing a fist into his mouth, as if battling a terrible toothache.

Running out of the park, he scurried home, skunklike, to a handful of sedatives from the medicine cabinet. Not counting the pills, he swallowed them and passed out.

He awoke at midnight, still shaking like a scared scarecrow. The inexplicable impulse was gone—but what if the compulsion overwhelmed him again?

He reached for the pills, recalling that the year before, a counterrevolutionary had been executed in the People's Square for the crime of splashing a bottle of red ink on a statue of Chairman Mao, an accident that had appeared to the Red Guards as an atrocious crime of assassinating the great leader—symbolically.

What if he did not have easy access to the pills the next time?

He decided to carry, in a green plastic wallet, a packet of sedatives hidden behind Jianyin's picture. It would appear natural for him to touch the picture time and again—to make sure of the tranquilizer still being there, available through her gaze.

To his dismay, the picture soon turned yellow, either through some chemical reaction to the pills or from the constant touch of his sweaty hand. It seemed a portentous sign.

He eventually began to recover, but he did not really regain any confidence—not until after the death of Mao later that year. No one in school mentioned the incomplete poem again. It would be too ironic to chant, "A long life to Mao, a long, long life." He still carried the wallet with the hidden pills, though he no longer worried about a nervous breakdown. The picture turned increasingly yellow with time, looking almost like a remnant from another life, and he failed to bring himself closer to Jianyin in person. Nor could he admit to her that he had picked up the picture and still had it with him. Their relationship seemed to have been framed in the plastic picture pocket.

Then one chilly winter day, the wallet was stolen. For weeks, Peng was devastated, until he found a cold comfort in a thought: to the pickpocket, the pills, long pulverized, must have looked like drying material, to protect a still precious picture.

A Jing Dynasty Goat

(1979)

This is the last issue of *Red Dust Lane Blackboard Newsletter* for the year 1979, an important and eventful year for our country. In January, China established diplomatic relations with the United States. Comrade Deng Xiaoping visited the United States and held talks with President Carter. In February, Chinese frontier troops launched a counter-attack against Vietnamese aggressors in the Guangxi and Yunnan frontier zones and won great victories. In April, with the goal of four modernizations of our country in mind, Deng Xiaoping enumerated the four cardinal principles: keeping to the socialist road, upholding the proletarian dictatorship, upholding the leadership of the Communist Party, and upholding Marxism-Leninism and Mao Zedong thought. The CPC Central Committee and the State Council ratified four special economic zones in Guangdong and Fujian. At the celebration of the thirtieth anniversary of the founding of the People's Republic of

China, Comrade Ye Jianying recalled the great achievements of the Chinese Party and people since liberation in
1949 and presented a self-criticism of the Party's mistakes
during the Cultural Revolution.

After twenty-one years' imprisonment, Jiang Xiaoming was
suddenly released on a July morning.

The Party secretary of the Shanghai No. 1 Prison, high-
buttoned as usual, in a spic-and-span gray wool Mao suit,
explained the higher authorities' decision.

"It is the right decision to release you in 1979, Comrade
Jiang," the Party secretary said, with all the imaginable
sincerity in his official tone. "It was a mistake to put you
into prison in 1957, during the anti-bourgeois-rightist movement, but you ought to be grateful to the Communist Party
for its great policy. When we recognize a mistake, we correct it. Otherwise, you could have remained in that dark
cell all your life. So, you start a new life today. Go back to
your home in Red Dust Lane. We have contacted the neighborhood committee there, and the room is still there under
your name, waiting for you."

In addition, the Party secretary gave Jiang five hundred
yuan as a kind of compensation for these lost years in prison.

As accustomed to being a rightist as a snail is to carrying its house on its back, Jiang was befuddled. In 1957, Mao
had called on intellectuals to speak out like "a hundred
flowers blossoming together," and Jiang, a young teacher

who had just published a history book, talked about the contingency of history in a department meeting. Then, all of a sudden, he was thrown in jail as a rightist, for the crime of denying the ultimate role of the proletariat in making history. He had since lost his ability to tell the difference between night and day, let alone analyze historical and social changes, having lived in a dark prison cell, like a lone bat.

It was a hot, bright morning outside of the high walls. He blinked in the sunlight. The street looked so different. One block away, there was a fancy store with a dazzling display of summer fashions in its windows—a line of mannequins dressed in skinny-strap, tulip-cup necklines and brief-and-halter combinations . . . as if from a Hollywood movie scene. He rubbed his eyes.

According to an old Chinese saying, "Seven days in a high mountain cave, and a thousand years has elapsed down in the mundane world." Jiang shook his head. A red convertible sped by, from which a young girl in a yellow summer dress looked at him curiously, a pug dog sitting on her lap. It was another scene he had never before witnessed.

After wandering about for two hours in a maze of traffic, floundering along the new roads and the old roads he could hardly recognize, making one wrong turn after another, finally he found himself approaching a used bookstore close to Red Dust Lane.

He was not eager to go back to the lane. The attic room might still be there, but so much had changed. *How much sorrow do you have? / Like the spring water of a long, long river flowing east!* Some long-forgotten lines were coming back to him. The prospect of him, an ex-rightist, reporting to the neighborhood committee seemed anything but pleasant.

So he stepped into the bookstore, which was tiny, yet impressively stacked with books. The store appeared to have been converted from a residential room. With the wear and tear of so many years, his memory failed to register whose room it could have been.

He was surprised to see a bikini girl on a poster marked "For Sale" near the entrance. In his memory, such a poster would have been condemned as bourgeois decadence. "For Sale" was also a new term for him. Fixed prices were said to be one advantage of the socialist system. Even this bookstore was bewilderingly different.

There were so many new books. He could not understand some of the titles—even those in the field he had taught. He searched around for a while without finding anything he wanted to read. Then he recognized a piece of melody that came rippling across the store, Tchaikovsky's String Quartet no. 1. He also heard a baby's babble behind a bamboo-bead curtain at the back.

To his astonishment, he came upon three copies of his study on the contingency of history under the bikini girl poster.

Taking a deep breath, he took them to the counter. A young man with a thick mustache, apparently the owner of the store, said with a scholarly air, "You surely have an eye for books, sir. They'll be six hundred and thirty yuan."

"What?" Jiang gasped. "The original price is less than two yuan."

"It was criticized as a counterrevolutionary attack against the Party in the fifties," the owner said. "Out of print for many years. A collectable item. We got hold of them through a special channel."

"How?"

When Jiang had been snatched away from home, hand-cuffed, there were several copies of the book left behind. His wife had said that she would wait for his return, keeping all the books, though it was the books that had gotten him into the trouble.

"You will not be able to find it in any other bookstores in Shanghai." The owner did not answer his question directly. "A very special channel."

Jiang grasped the books. "Look, young man. I wrote this book. And I have just come out—"

"Really?" The owner studied him for a long moment. "Oh, you must be Professor—all right, thirty, that's the price we paid. Welcome back to Red Dust Lane. The poster is free for you."

Jiang took the books without accepting the additional offer. There was a small scar on the bikini girl's bare shoulder, which reminded him of his wife. She had died during his "rightist" years.

He started to leaf through the book as he continued on his way to Red Dust Lane, reading while walking being a habit he had formed in his pre-rightist years.

Emperor Yan is bored by the screens of naked bodies. In 266 he founded the Jing Dynasty, which resembles the previous Wei Dynasty in that His Majesty wields absolute power. All the emperor's men. And women too. There are so many imperial concubines that choosing is little better than a nightmare. He has a favorite goat. So he lets the goat amble before him through a sea of bedrooms. Wherever the goat stops, he takes it as Heaven's will that he spend the night in that room. More often than not, he finds the goat halting in front of the 311th concubine's pearl-curtained door. She is wrapped in a white cloud, naked beneath, in anticipation of the coming rain. She is not exactly beautiful, but when the candle is blown out, one body is not much different from another. She bears him a son who becomes Emperor Xing. Emperor Xing loses the country to barbarian aggressors through his thirst for a sea harbor. It is a long, complicated story, but the 311th concubine's secret is simple. According to an imprisoned historian, it consists of her sprinkling saltwater on the doorsteps. The goat, pampered as it is in the palace, stoops to lick the salt there. The moral is clear: a goat is a goat.

Uniform

(1980)

This is the last issue of *Red Dust Lane Blackboard Newsletter* for the year 1980. Our Party and our people have made great progress, recovering from the national disaster of ten years—the Cultural Revolution. China was admitted to the International Monetary Fund and the World Bank. The Fifth Session of the Eleventh CPC Central Committee elected Hu Yaobang general secretary of the Party, and then Zhao Ziyang replaced Hua Guofeng as premier. Deng Xiaoping and other revolutionaries of the older generation resigned due to age. The Gang of Four and several others were tried and convicted for their crimes during the Cultural Revolution. China joined the World Intellectual Property Organization as it ninetieth member.

Sometimes, the beginning of a story is so wonderful that you may simply wish, "Oh that's the story," like Othello's exclamation upon Desdemona's arrival, but then the story goes on, in an unexpected direction. In retrospect, there is only one thing you can do: focus as much as possible on what you think of as the most memorable. And that's the beginning, in the year of 1980.

In 1980, like a Yellow River carp jumping through the Dragon Gate, I left Red Dust Lane in Shanghai and became a graduate student at Beijing Foreign Language University.

I was disappointed, however, at the living conditions in the dorm room. Four students had to squeeze in a single room only fifteen square meters in size. With three bunk beds, two desks, and a bookshelf made of boards and bricks, there was hardly any space left to move around. But that was shortly after the end of the Cultural Revolution, and people were full of hopes and passions for a new beginning. We studied hard for the "realization of four modernizations," the four of us sweating in the small dorm room.

That year, Qi, one of the four, started dating Mimi, a young army doctor stationed in Tong County. A delicious girl with a watermelon-seed-shaped face, almond-long eyes, and cherry lips, she spoke in a voice as sweet as freshly peeled lychee, bringing "a fresh breeze full of the orchard fragrance" to our stuffy room.

"So fruity," Little Zhao commented at night. "As Confucius says, so luscious you could devour."

"The grapes are sweetly ripe in Tulufan . . ." I hummed, echoing a then-popular song.

"Apple blossom blazing transparent in a dream," Old Ke said, swallowing a handful of sleeping pills. Ke was the only roommate who was married. His wife worked in Jiangsu province, about five hundred miles away from Beijing.

Qi smiled in response. The lights were out, so we could not see his smile, but we knew. After a long day's work, sleep did not come easily in our dorm room. To unwind, we would talk in the dark, and one of the most rewarding topics was Mimi. All those "fruity" epithets were the combined product of our evening conversation, partially in reference to her family origin, as her parents worked in a state-run orchard, but more in recognition of the freshness that she infused into our lives.

It was hot that year. She came wearing her summer clothes, each time a different blaze of colors, mostly in a style called *Bulajie*, sometimes sleeveless, sometimes with thin straps.

Minutes after her arrival, we would head out of the dorm and to the library, leaving Qi and Mimi alone.

One afternoon, she stopped us. "I've made something for all of you." She kicked off her shoes, climbed on to the long desk, and put a new pillow cover on my pillow on the upper bunk. Standing on the desk, she appeared tall, slender, her scarlet-painted toes prettier than rose petals in the sunlight. She did the same on Qi's bed. As she stepped down, Old Ke took the next pillow cover from her and spread it himself. Little Zhao hastened to do the same.

Before leaving the room, Little Zhao whispered to me that he couldn't help taking an extra look or two at her in her summer dress—her pink face as fresh as the hibiscus out of water, her legs as white as the lotus root in the lake, her toes as round as peeled longan . . . A delicious heart as well as a dazzling body, we all agreed.

Qi seemed to think differently, however, as he said with frost in his voice, "I told you to come in your army uniform. How could you have forgotten again?"

We were puzzled. How could Qi be that grouchy? A glance at Mimi in the summer was like ice cream to us— but to our eyes only.

"What's the matter with you, Qi?" Little Zhao asked during the night talk in our dorm room. "You must be so old-fashioned. You would be happy seeing her wrapped head to foot like a mummy, wouldn't you?"

"No, you are wrong," Qi replied. "She is far more beautiful in her uniform."

"You are sick, Qi." I took Little Zhao's side. "How could that possibly be?"

"It's so hot." Old Ke put in one of his rare comments.

Not that we had any objection, political or otherwise, to the sight of people wearing their uniforms. We simply failed to imagine anything attractive about Mimi in her uniform: baggy pants, baggy jacket, drab green color from head to foot, and her curves all lost in the overall shapelessness.

The next Saturday, she came in her uniform as Qi had requested. It was a sweltering day. With no air-conditioning or electric fan in our room, she perspired profusely. The uniform was stuck to her back and front, crumpled out of shape. She had traveled all the way in an overcrowded bus, her black hair falling limp out of her red-starred cap.

"I could not take a seat on the bus," she said, fanning herself with a literature magazine, "because of my uniform."

"Why?" I asked.

"Whenever someone old or small gets on the bus," she said, "you're supposed to give your seat away—as a PLA soldier."

The image of Comrade Lei Feng, a selfless Communist soldier in the sixties, still remained fresh in people's memory in the early eighties.

"It is such a scorching hot day," Little Zhao observed, shaking his head, "for you to wear your stuffy uniform."

"But you look so beautiful today," Qi said, his face glowing with infatuation.

We were all confused and enraged as we walked out of the dorm room.

One night the following week, Qi went to a concert with Mimi in her uniform. To punish him, I used his hair growth medicine to fuel an alcohol stove to make scrambled eggs. To my surprise, they were the best scrambled eggs I had ever tasted. Little Zhao then came up with more practical jokes, and they began to unsettle Qi. About a week later, by way of explanation, Qi told us a story about himself.

"In the early seventies, it was my dream to be a PLA solider, a dream like the high floating moon, upon which I hung my hopes. It was like being politically gold-plated in socialist China."

"That's true," Old Ke cut in. "Once enlisted, young people did not have to worry about being caught up in the movement of the educated youths going to the country-side. Military service would also secure them state-run company jobs after their discharge."

Though I was Qi's junior by three or four years, I understood. The status of a PLA soldier spoke volumes during the Cultural Revolution. It was like a shining stamp of political reliability, sending one far into the promising future.

"As soon as I turned eighteen, I turned in my application," Qi went on. "I was disqualified, however, because of my family background. My parents were professors—'black monsters' during the Cultural Revolution. As a result, my schoolmates treated me like trash—like a 'black puppy.' A green army uniform was like an unreachable oasis in my dreams."

"So it's a sort of substitution or compensation," I observed after Qi left the room to go to the dorm phone in the corridor. "Qi is fulfilling his dream by having Mimi walk beside him in her uniform, arm in arm. In those moments, all the humiliation of those years vanish."

"It's perhaps more than that," Little Zhao said, trying to be profound. "It is the contrast between her military appearance and her submissive reality. As Confucius says, a woman makes herself beautiful for the man who has fallen for her—in her uniform or not."

Old Ke raised a question instead: "Would he have fallen for her—if she was not in her uniform?"

But we were too busy to worry about hypothetical questions. Time flowed like water; soon we were overwhelmed by our preparations for our dissertations, and then for the defense. We moved out of the dorm, going our different ways after graduation. I got a job in Shanghai. Old Ke became an executive at one of the earliest American-Chinese joint ventures. Little Zhao was offered a position at a research institute. Qi remained at the university.

Qi wrote me that he had married Mimi, enclosing a picture taken in the Summer Palace: Qi in his Polo T-shirt, Mimi in her sweat-soaked uniform. There was one short sentence at the back of the picture:

"My Polo is fake, but her uniform is genuine."

Shortly afterward, Qi went to the United States to further his studies, and Mimi followed. They had a son there. We wrote less and less to each other although we always spoke of visiting. I, too, got married, though not to someone in the army. It no longer seemed so desirable or fashionable for a young woman to be seen in her uniform. The economic reform launched by Deng Xiaoping in the mid-eighties began to offer a lot of new opportunities for people.

After a couple more years, I made up my mind to study at an American university. Once I arrived in the United States, I got in touch with Qi again, who had been teaching in a small college in the east.

During my spring break, I decided to visit Qi for the reunion much anticipated in our correspondence. It was not until two days before the trip, however, that I learned Qi had divorced.

"Mimi is no longer with me," Qi mumbled over the phone.

"What?"

"I'll tell you more when you get here, OK?"

The trip took longer than I had expected. I got lost several times on the way. My wife did a lot of complaining, along with the sputtering engine of the fifteen-year-old Mazda, before we finally pulled up to the bleak old house Qi had bought.

"It's so easy to be judgmental, but not everything in this world works out as we planned," Qi said, shaking his head over the Oolong tea, in a subtle reference to his divorce.

"I understand," I said, chewing a tea leaf, not as eager to judge as in those years back in Beijing. "As an ancient sage says, 'Eight or nine out of ten times, things go wrong in this world of ours.'"

In the late afternoon, Qi prepared a barbeque for us in his backyard. The ribs sizzled deliciously over the grill made from an antique tank. After a short while, my wife went back into the living room with a platter of meat to watch her favorite TV program. Qi and I remained sitting outside in a corner overgrown with weeds and enveloped in smoke. Cicadas started chirping, distantly, and different from those in Beijing. Against the rugged mountain lines, the sun on the back of a wild goose seemed to be coloring a corner of the enflamed sky.

"It's a long story," Qi said, turning a rib over on the grill with a pair of mahogany chopsticks. "I considered myself lucky to get a job in this small town, but there was no job for her here. Her command of English was not good enough to pass the medical license test. In fact, she couldn't even disclose her army experience, as it would be a disadvantage in applying for jobs here. Her temper gradually soured and she finally snapped like a frostbitten twig. She's no longer the one we knew in Beijing."

No longer the one in the uniform—like "a fresh breeze full of the orchard fragrance." The half-forgotten phrase almost jumped to my tongue, but I did not say it. Nor could I bring myself to ask him any specific questions about their divorce.

After the ribs, we shared a wooden bowl of peeled longan in syrup, which was supposed to benefit both yin and yang in the human body. It was a rarity here, even though no longer fresh.

Instead, I asked if he had some recent pictures of her. He hesitated before taking out a photo album. Among the pictures was one of Mimi working in a Chinese restaurant. She was still handsome, though I detected fatigue in the lines around her eyes. She wore a scarlet silk restaurant uniform—a sleeveless mandarin dress with high slits revealing her shapely legs and ivory thighs. An oriental attraction among the Western customers, presumably.

"In Boston," he said in a subdued voice. "She found a job in a Chinese restaurant. My son brought the picture back."

"By the wine urn, the girl is like the moon, / her white wrists like frost, like snow." On impulse, I quoted a couplet from Wei Zhuang's "Reminiscence of the South." I immediately regretted the exuberance, which sounded totally out of time and place.

"Except we are no longer young," he responded, referencing the last two lines of that famous poem: *Still young, I am not going back home, / or I'll have a broken heart.*

Sighing, he took off his wig. To my astonishment, he was completely bald, his skull shining in the afternoon sunlight, like a cooked egg. I suddenly recalled the practical joke in the Beijing dorm room—the hair growth medicine and the scrambled eggs . . . It was as though all that had happened in another world, the weakening flames of memory burning in the tiny alcohol stove.

It was not the reunion I had imagined. We lost touch again, though I knew he still taught there.

Last night, I was awakened by a sound like a black night bird flapping violently against the window in Red Dust

Lane. It turned out to be an unexpected call from Little Zhao in Beijing.

"Mimi came back to Beijing. She had a hard time finding a job there, with no competitive skills in the tough job market of the late nineties. A middle-aged woman, her face sunk like a dried orange, she looks as thin as a bamboo stick in an old-fashioned padded army coat that few would wear nowadays. She went to Old Ke, who is now a Big Buck in Beijing, but he offered no help."

Disoriented at this eerie hour, I knew I could not fall asleep again. So I got up and searched through the shelves before coming upon a volume of W. B. Yeats, remembering something the poet once said about a tattered coat upon a stick. Instead, I found a couple of different lines in "Easter 1916," in which the poet lamented, *"Being certain that they and I / But lived where motley is worn."*

It may be the clothes that make us what we are, and not the other way around, whether motley or uniform.

Still, I tried to focus on the memory, in that far away summer, when Qi in his fake Polo T-shirt and Mimi in her sweat-soaked uniform smiled together in the zoom lens of somebody's camera.

Big Bowl and Firecracker

(1984)

This is the last issue of *Red Dust Lane Blackboard Newsletter* for the year 1984. It has been a year of great success and achievement for our country. In January, Chinese Premier Zhao Ziyang visited the United States, and then American President Ronald Reagan visited China in April. The Party authorities stressed two major tasks for the country in the new period: restructuring the economy and opening the country to the outside world. Deng Xiaoping made the solemn promise that Hong Kong's socioeconomic system would remain the same after its return to China: "One country, two systems." In December, British Prime Minister Margaret Thatcher and Premier Zhao signed the Sino-British Joint Declaration on the return of Hong Kong in 1997.

Xie Zhengmin had got his nickname—Big Bowl—when his family moved from Jin'an district into Red Dust Lane in 1967, the second year of the Cultural Revolution. He was then only ten.

He immediately learned about the culture of the lane. Most families had no air-conditioning or electric fans at home, and in the summer, it was almost unbearable to have a hot meal inside. There was no traffic in the lane, and a pleasant, fitful breeze rippled through, so people came out holding their rice bowls, eating heartily in the open. It was a sort of social occasion for the lane. Talking and laughing, one would put a piece of soy sauce–braised lamb into his friend's bowl in return for half of a smoked fish head. Such exchanges were particularly common among kids.

So Xie Zhengmin also chose to eat outside. His nickname might have originated from the extraordinarily big bowl in his hands. There were those who thought there was more to it, though. Instead of mixing with the other kids, he stood aloof in a corner, as if burying his face in that big bowl. What was the point of eating outside if you were going to eat like that? The nickname could have been a reference to that puzzle.

Whatever the origin, the nickname stuck. Big Bowl's younger brother got his by association—Small Bowl—and then their parents got nicknames too. The mother was called Bamboo Chopsticks, because she was so thin, and the father was Steamed Bun, because he looked a little fermented.

In the evening talk of the lane, people didn't care so much about those nicknames, but there was something suspicious about the Xies. In the city of Shanghai, location mattered a lot. Red Dust Lane, though at the center of Huangpu district, was not considered an upper-class area. The *shikumen* houses here had been built with neither gas nor bathroom facilities, so early in the morning, the housewives had to start a fire in their coal briquette stoves by waving palm leaf fans like robots and had to carry out the chamber pots with sleepy eyes. In contrast, Jin'an district was a higher-class area. That the Xies had moved from there to a pathetic two-room combination here—an attic and a *tingzijian* cubicle over the kitchen—was too much of a bad bargain not to arouse comment.

It wasn't long before the answer came. Steamed Bun had become a target for the neighborhood criticism meeting in Jin'an district, and he had been forced to wear around his neck a blackboard that showed his class status: Stinking Capitalist. As a capitalist, he and his family members were viewed as "black"—politically unreliable—and subject to revolutionary discrimination in the neighborhood.

But it was useless for them to move. The Red Guards from Steamed Bun's company followed them over to Red Dust Lane, putting a bunch of slogan papers and posters on their door and windows: *Down with stinking capitalist*.

Indeed, the proletarian dictatorship was everywhere. The neighborhood committee of Red Dust Lane, too, held a mass-criticism meeting against the Xies.

The Xies did not move anymore. Big Bowl hung his head lower in the lane, with or without the bowl. *"No face,"* an elderly neighbor said, pointing out the symbolic meaning of the gesture. "That's why the boy has been hiding his face in the big bowl since his arrival."

Face or no face, Big Bowl grew up like others. In the late seventies, the Cultural Revolution was officially declared a national disaster, and the class system was practically shelved. Big Bowl started to greet his neighbors amiably, holding his head high. There were other changes in the lane too. People did not eat outside as much, since more and more families bought electric fans.

Big Bowl became a young accountant for a state-run company. According to Bamboo Chopsticks, he took evening college courses, turned in his application for Party membership, and went to Beijing several times as a representative of the company. In short, he was a young man with a promising future.

Soon we saw him bringing a young girl surnamed Qian into the lane. She worked at the same company, though it was said that their relationship faced challenges. In the once popular class system, Qian's father was a worker, and their families did not match, politically. While it was difficult to tell what Qian saw in Big Bowl, it was not so difficult to understand the reverse. Qian was very pretty, and Big Bowl went out of his way to introduce her to his neighbors.

The class difference was no longer considered that important, not like it was back in the days when Big Bowl had first acquired his nickname. Things had changed in China, the way colorful balls rotate through a juggler's hands. Now people actually found there were benefits to a black family background. Some of those families got compensation for their losses during the Cultural Revolution. Some were able to reestablish contact with relatives overseas, which often meant a sizable amount of money coming to them from abroad. Big Bowl, it turned out, had a rich uncle in the United States.

In the second year of their relationship, the young couple began discussing their marriage plans, but Bamboo Chopsticks started to complain in the lane. "Qian's family has nothing. The revolutionary proletariat indeed. We have to pay for everything."

Qian's family, it was said, was not happy either. The issue of family background aside, where was the "wedding room" for the young couple? Big Bowl's family remained huddled together in that two-room combination—an attic and a cubicle above the kitchen—and in the best scenario, the young couple would get one of the two.

"To marry into such a capitalist family," Old Qian, the young girl's father, admonished her, "is like having the smell of the fish, but not getting any of the meat."

"Some people simply cannot resist the smell!" Bamboo Chopsticks declared at the lane entrance when she heard, stamping her feet as though in a loyal character dance.

But it was no longer the time of arranged marriages.

The two young people remained adamant, and the parents on both sides could do little to change their minds.

So the wedding was scheduled for the summer. Most of the neighbors in the lane got small bags of happiness candies, including two chocolate coins wrapped in gold paper. Some also received a wedding invitation. Big Bowl's parents had reserved more than thirty tables at the Guoji Hotel, one of the top restaurants in Shanghai. At the rate of eight hundred yuan per table, it would cost about twenty-five thousand yuan—more than Old Qian's income for ten years—not to mention the other expenses. But the lane had another way to calculate the cost. In China's time of economic reform, the most practical and popular wedding presents came in the form of cash in a red envelope. The current standard gift was a hundred yuan per person, and some honored guests—those at the table with the bride and bridegroom—could pay up to five hundred yuan. With ten to twelve people per table, if each and every guest was as decent as expected, such a grand wedding might even turn a profit. No one could be sure, though. Some cheap guys might put in only twenty yuan in a red envelope.

"It's a capitalist wedding," Old Qian grumbled. He was an ex-member of the Mao Zedong Thought Propaganda Team, who still flourished a couple of political terms like his metal tooth. "Nothing but exploitation."

"It's a wedding," Bamboo Chopsticks countered, spitting out the husk of a watermelon seed. "If they don't need face, we have to have ours."

It seemed like a sound argument in the changed times. During the Cultural Revolution, people had simple, cost-effective weddings based on the principle of following the Party's tradition of hard work and a simple life. Nowadays such a practice would make laughingstocks of the young couple.

A tough negotiation was staged between the two families. Conventionally, the two sides would share the cost, but Old Qian had recently suffered a pay cut at his factory. It was finally agreed that the groom's family would be responsible for all costs and, in exchange, only two banquet tables would be allocated to the bride's family and friends.

"It's an unbelievable bargain for them," Bamboo Chopsticks concluded with a chuckle. "They can pocket the red envelopes from those two tables. A huge profit out of the thin air."

Her continuous "news conference" kept the lane informed of all the progress up to the day of the wedding. When that day arrived, the lane held its breath in excitement. Cameras flashed at the dowry of twelve silk quilts piled high in front of the door, at the red paper cut designs put on the windows, and at the Red Flag limousine at the lane entrance, a special automobile that had allegedly chauffeured Chairman Mao in the sixties.

We wondered what the wedding at the celebrated Guoji Hotel would be like, and we waited eagerly to hear. Before the banquet was finished, Small Bowl hurried back to the lane, to prepare for the young couple's homecoming. His face flushed the color of a red cloth, he declared that it was an unprecedented wedding.

"Eight cold dishes. Eight hot dishes. Four big platters. The whole duck. The whole chicken. The whole fish. The whole Jinhua ham. Two soups. Not to mention four desserts. The banquet lasted more than three hours. The bride and bridegroom had to walk around to each and every table, with cups in their hands. The guests kept toasting to their happiness, and the young couple, especially the bridegroom, had to drink to their toasts or the guests would lose face. So I had to act as the wine guard, drinking on his behalf. It would be a shame for the bridegroom to get drunk tonight. Indeed, one minute in the wedding room is worth tons of gold."

Small Bowl then brought out a pile of firecrackers, arranging for some to be set off at the lane entrance; some, at the center of the lane; and the rest to be set off by himself in front of the *shikumen* door. It was considered auspicious for the couple, and the more firecrackers, the better luck.

Upon the Red Flag limousine's arrival, the whole lane was overwhelmed by a joyful outburst of firecrackers.

Now, there's no story without coincidence.

As the bride was stepping into the house, the long bunch of firecrackers in Small Bowl's hand failed to explode.

"This one is rotten," Small Bowl grumbled in the awkward silence that instantly shrouded the air. "Let's start a new one."

"What? What do you mean?" Old Qian exploded. "You cannot be humiliating us like that."

"Come on. It is only a bad firecracker. You know the quality of those products nowadays."

"A bad firecracker at the moment my daughter steps into your home as the bride? It's not just humiliating, but downright unlucky too."

"How can you say that today?" Bamboo Chopsticks shot up like a firecracker herself. "Your mouth needs to be cleaned thoroughly with a chamber pot broom!"

"Damn you, you black-hearted-and-black-lunged capitalist wife," Old Qian shouted, as if miraculously transported back to the days of the Cultural Revolution, a white-haired working-class rebel cursing in front of a door decorated with red signs of happiness. "You are good at nothing except exploiting people. How much have you made from the red envelopes? We working class are still the leading class in socialist China. Don't you forget that!"

"What have you done, you old idiot?" Small Bowl was furious. "You have not paid a single penny out of your own pocket. You are the cheapest dirt."

"Nobody did it on purpose," Steamed Bun said. "It was only because of the quality of the firecrackers."

"The quality?" Old Qian went on relentlessly. "Couldn't you have chosen something better? You have money, don't you? How dare you to treat my daughter like dirt! Yes, we are working-class people, but we won't save money on the firecrackers for the wedding."

Now all the neighbors poured out to watch the scene. They tried to calm down both sides, but without success. Apparently, the firecracker was only the fuse that finally set off the long pent-up feud between the two sides. It was clear that nobody—except perhaps the bride and bridegroom, who had already evaporated into their room— would be able to put an end to the fight.

But the couple did not come out.

They might not have heard it at first, but when no one followed them into the wedding room, the couple should have noticed. It was a time-honored convention that the guests would "celebrate by turning the wedding room upside down." No one in the street, however, paid any attention to the ritual, what with the increasingly intense drama of the brawl.

Finally, in the middle of the chaos, Big Bowl came rushing out, pushing his way through the crowd, striding toward the lane exit, shouting with both arms raised above his head.

"You all can shut up now. Everything is finished. I've killed her. Now I'm turning myself in to the police bureau."

People were stunned into silence. It did not look like he was making a joke—a very bad one—but no one could believe it. Old Qian was transfixed with his fist banging at the air, as if turned into a stone statue by a magic spell. Small Bowl was the first to get his wits back, sprinting up to the wedding room, while the others remained standing there in the lane, too shocked and stupefied to react.

Comrade Jun, the head of the neighborhood committee, arrived at the scene, and an outburst of voices rocketed up like firecrackers trying to explain. "A life for a firecracker!"

Small Bowl ran back down again, shouting, "Wait! Big Bowl! Don't go there!"

Then Qian stumbled down, her hair disheveled, her clothes in terrible disarray, screaming, running barefoot. "Come back, Big Bowl!"

The crowd gasped. "She's—a ghost! Wait—she's not dead."

But it was already too late.

When the bride dashed into the police station, the bridegroom had already signed the statement saying that he had strangled his wife in a fit of fury. It was too humiliating that his father-in-law had made a scene on his wedding day, and that she, too, screamed like a fury in the wedding room. He had lost all face, and his faith too, in a marriage with such an ugly start. And he lost control of himself temporarily.

Now, Big Bowl couldn't be charged with homicide, since the victim was not dead, but nonetheless, it was an attempted homicide. The statement lay on the desk, signed, in black and white. Big Bowl was thrown into custody. It then became a matter of the uttermost urgency to prove that the statement made by Big Bowl was not true.

Qian told a different story. According to her, it was not his fault at all. When they first heard the noise outside, he wanted her to stop her father. She didn't want to. Instead, she started to scream and scratch at him like a fury. The fight in the wedding room only added fuel to the fire. He tried to keep her from making things worse by putting his hand over her mouth. She struggled so violently that she lost consciousness.

The following morning, she further amended her statement by insisting that she fainted because she had been too exhausted by all the preparations for the wedding, including the purchase of all the firecrackers, which she had personally chosen at a market. It really had nothing to do with him at all.

Whose side was credible—the bride's or the bridegroom's?

How it had happened that night in the wedding room, we didn't know, but we chose to believe her story. After all, it's a bad firecracker's luck.

When the police came to the lane to investigate, Comrade Jun offered an interpretation from his own experience.

"Big Bowl was drunk that night. You cannot take a drunken man's word for it. As the head of the neighborhood committee, I've dealt with too many people who were in the cup. Do you know how many cups he drank that night? Now, I'm always against this kind of lavish wedding, but they didn't listen to me. It is difficult for us to do the neighborhood work nowadays, comrades."

Those neighbors who had attended the banquet at the Guoji Hotel supported this by testifying that Big Bowl had consumed more than ten cups of sorghum liquor. Qian was more credible, they further argued, since she had hardly had a drop that night.

Big Bowl's company, too, put in a good word for him. He had been an honest, hardworking accountant. The fact that he had turned himself in spoke for itself. Even drunk, he remained a law-abiding citizen. The predicament of Qian was also brought up in the discussion. If anything happened to him, what would happen to her—waiting for him for so many years in Red Dust Lane, like the Beijing opera heroine Wang Baochuan?

When Big Bowl was released in October, Qian was about three months pregnant.

Red Dust Lane was once more abuzz with stories and speculations.

Now, the time from the moment that Old Qian and Bamboo Chopsticks started fighting in the lane to the moment when Big Bowl ran out was about forty-five minutes. We calculated closely. What could the bride and bridegroom have done during the forty-five minutes when they were alone in the wedding room? All the details—that she came out barefoot, her hair disheveled, her clothes in disarray—spoke for themselves. But others had different versions. The young couple must have heard the fight outside from the very beginning. How could they have been in the mood? So it must have happened before the wedding.

The humiliation of having fought with his wife and turned himself in for a false murder on his wedding day, plus gossip in the lane about the circumstance of Qian's pregnancy, proved to be too much.

Once again Big Bowl hung his head low, as if he were suffering from a broken neck, just the way he had when he had first moved in and buried his face in a big bowl.

Fortunately, his uncle had mailed a large sum from the United States, Bamboo Chopsticks announced proudly in the lane. According to the new policy, overseas Chinese could buy their apartments in the city with foreign currency. So the young couple was soon going to move out of Red Dust Lane to a new apartment.

There, we hoped, they would be able to start a new life.

A Confidence Cap

(1987)

This is the last issue of *Red Dust Lane Blackboard Newsletter* for the year 1987. In the beginning of the year, the Party authorities launched the campaign to fight against bourgeois liberalism under Western influence and accepted Hu Yaobang's resignation from the post of general secretary of the Party Central Committee. In October, in the CPC National Congress, Zhao Ziyang gave the report "Advance along the Road of Socialism with Chinese Characteristics," stating that the basic role of the Party during the primary stage of socialism is to lead people in an effort to turn China into a prosperous, strong, democratic, culturally advanced, and modern socialist country by making economic development the Party's central task while adhering to the four cardinal principles and persevering in reform and open policy. With such an important document to guide China's reform, the Chinese people are full of confidence for the great future of the country. Of course, there can be twists and turns in our advances; of this we are well aware, and the Party authorities took decisive and effective measures against widespread corruption in the system. This year, an agreement between China and Portugal was signed calling for the return of Macao to China in 1999.

Twenty years had passed like a snapping of one's fingers, Fu Guodong thought, standing hatless, shivering in the cold wind outside the university conference hall. However, he had never thought about buying himself a hat, since that winter night in 1966.

That long-ago night, at the beginning of the Cultural Revolution, he had witnessed his sick father wearing a tall white paper hat bearing big Chinese characters: *Down with the black bourgeois authority, American secret agent.* The old man was a college professor who had studied in the United States and had come back in the fifties as an authority in physics, and he was turned into a black target for the Red Guards in the sixties. A young boy, Fu himself was turned into a "black puppy," having to support his sick father as he stood on the mass-criticism stage near the entrance of Red Dust Lane. There he saw the tall paper hat on his father's head trembling in the howling wind as some sort of pale sign from the underworld.

His father passed away shortly afterward, though his "political hat" still cast a shadow over the family, particularly Fu. It was a shadow not removed until several years after the Cultural Revolution, when Fu became a college student at the university where his father had taught. Four years later, as if through another stroke of ironic causality of misplaced yin and yang, he started teaching there too.

He did not dream of becoming an authority like his father. *Once bitten by a snake, a man turns panicky at the sight of a coiled black rope.* With that evening wind still howling in his memory, he seemed incapable of "warming up." And his subject happened to be a "cold" one too: comparative linguistics, with a focus on the etymology of the Chinese language. Still, in the lane, a college teacher was somebody, and everyone expected that, sooner or later, he would move out.

But Fu was a contented man, with a stable income and occasional extra money from his academic publications, so he had no immediate plans to move. He kept a low profile in the lane. Whenever addressed as Professor, he would insist that he was still a lecturer. In the one single room inherited from his father, he piled up books—he was indeed a bookworm, about whom there was nothing too surprising. His continuous celibacy in his mid-thirties, for instance, was easily attributed to his bookishness. He copied out a couplet by Zhuge Liang on a long silk scroll, which he then hung on the wall: *It is enough for a man to survive in an age of troubles; it is vain to seek one's name among the glorious.*

However low his profile, he worked diligently and published copiously in his field. In time, his name spread beyond the college and outside the country as well. As in the proverb, a red apricot tree could not help blossoming over the wall.

Now, on the present winter evening in the late eighties, as he stood outside of the university conference hall thinking back on the scene twenty years earlier, he was hit with a weird sense of déjà vu. He had just delivered a talk at an international culture conference on campus. The session on comparative linguistics had been attended by a number of well-known Western scholars: there had been a recent revival of interest worldwide in the Chinese language as a system of ideograms, and Chinese characters had become so fashionable that they were appearing on T-shirts and as tattoos. Fu's speech focused on Ezra Pound's deconstruction of ancient Chinese characters into poetic images, and Fu demonstrated his groundbreaking insight into the subject. His talk was well received, and afterward, Professor Allen, from an American university, and Professor Hornbeck, from a German university, insisted on treating him to dinner.

While out with the two, Fu kept shivering, even though he was sandwiched between the Western scholars in a taxi. It was a chilly rainy evening.

The two foreigners exchanged glances, then had the taxi pull onto West Nanjing Road and dragged him into a brand-named store, where they proposed to pick out a cap for him. They recommended a brown wool flat cap, which was made in London and had a staggering price tag. Professor Hornbeck commented that its color suited his black hair perfectly. Professor Allen raved about its quality. Fu concurred, feeling he had no choice, even though the price was way beyond his ordinary budget. It would never do, he knew, for his Western colleagues to look down on their Chinese counterparts.

Wearing the cap, he went to the restaurant with them for a wonderful dinner of eight courses. The two foreigners kept raising their cups to his academic achievement. Halfway through the meal, he excused himself, and in the bathroom, he could not help studying his flushing face reflected in the mirror—a total stranger with an exotic British cap on his head.

The next morning, when he woke up, his first thoughts were about the cap. It was overcast outside. He wondered if it was feasible to wear it on campus. Considering the price he had paid for it, it would be a waste, he concluded, not to do so.

When he arrived on campus, he became aware that people were taking an extra look at him—or at the cap, which must have seemed out of character for the middle-aged, low-profile intellectual. No one could say, however, there was anything improper or wrong about it.

"You look like a person of authority," one of his female colleagues said, flashing him an ambiguous smile, "with such a cap on your head."

"Well, he is a person of authority," another colleague said as he arrived at Fu's side. "No question about it."

That was what the two Western scholars had said about him, Fu remembered, when they recommended the cap to him: they called him an authority in the field. After all, he had published more academic papers in international journals than most of his colleagues.

Anyway, it was a good, comfortable cap, providing a sort of warmth he had not experienced before. Soon, people got used to the sight of an oriental scholar on comparative linguistics walking around wearing an occidental cap. It was a cap that became him, a conclusion reached not only by his colleagues but by his neighbors in the lane too.

The following month, he spent a considerable sum for a pair of gold-rimmed glasses—to go with the cap.

And then, a new wool suit.

For all those years, he had spent little and saved enough that he could afford to go on a small-scale shopping spree.

Eventually, he became aware of the difference in himself—with the cap atop his head.

Spring came a couple of months later, and with it, the academic position discussion in the department at the university. Wearing the cap at the department office, he made a short yet surprising speech.

"In the last three years, I have published twenty-two papers in international journals. Among them, six have been quoted and mentioned by other scholars. If anyone in our department has published more in the field, he or she should be advanced to the full professorship. But if not, I should be the one," he concluded emphatically. "Several universities have contacted me."

The department heads gave serious thought to his statement. In the university ranking system recently introduced in China, the number of papers published abroad was one of the important considerations. Not only was he unmatched in publications, Fu was a good and hardworking teacher. Also, they were impressed by the unprecedented assertive tone in his speech, and they had to consider the possibility of his going to another university. They agreed unanimously to grant him full professorship.

Following this came the discussion of his housing assignment. As a full professor, Fu was qualified for better housing, so he was put at the top of the waiting list, even though it wasn't certain that an apartment key would be delivered to him anytime soon.

As a celebrated professor, he secured a prestigious state grant for his research project, which brought credit to the university as well. The grant was not exactly his money, but with it, he could carry out his work like never before, spending handsomely in the name of his research. Instead of squeezing into an overcrowded bus to the library, carrying a cold lunch box, he came and went by cab. Soon, he also had a young research assistant, who appeared in the lane from time to time. One evening, as they stepped into a taxi waiting for them at the front of the lane, she was seen grasping his hand.

"Remember that tall white paper hat his father wore during the Cultural Revolution? That was the worst luck imaginable, casting a shadow onto Fu as well," Old Root commented during the evening talk of Red Dust Lane. "He had to have something to cap it. Now look at that British cap. Brownish, almost purple—the purple *qi*. The purple luck from the West. That really caps it."

Housing Assignment

(1988)

This is the last issue of *Red Dust Lane Blackboard News-letter* for the year 1988.

In March, the National People's Congress discussed and approved the major tasks for the next five years for our country and elected new state leaders. In June and July, inflation hit double digits and prices soared. Shanghai, like some other large cities, experienced a wave of panic buying. The Party government decided to allow most commodity prices to be regulated by the markets, proposed various measures for improving the economic environment, and adopted the initial price and wage reform plan. This year also witnessed the beginning of the normalization of Sino-Soviet relations.

In the thirties, when the modern Chinese novelist Lao She wrote his well-known saga, *Four Generations under the Same*

Roof, such a large family was considered a blessing. It was in line with the time-honored tradition of Chinese civilization, as Liang Longhua argued, in which the old and young take care of each other in a family-based social structure.

But there was a fundamental difference during the eighties in China. The four generations in the novel lived in a large house, but Liang's family in Red Dust Lane lived under the ceiling of an all-purpose room of fourteen square meters in a *shikumen* house. The family members had to use curtain partitions to divide the room, which contained a bed for his grandfather; a bed for his parents; a bunk bed for his elder brother, his brother's wife, and their newborn baby; a foldable canvas bed for Liang himself; an all-purpose table serving as a dining table, desk, tea table, and ironing board; and, in a corner of the room, a chamber pot behind a plastic curtain. As in a Chinese proverb, people have to perform a Taoist mass in a snail shell.

The situation got even worse when, upon graduation from college, Liang was assigned a job at Shanghai Institute of Literature Studies. He desperately needed a room of his own, where he could concentrate on studying and researching. His family tried to behave as considerately as possible. The moment the dinner was over, they would clear the table and move out into the lane, so that he could write in peace and quiet. But even in the summer, it worked only for an hour or so. His grandfather had to listen to the radio, his parents to watch TV, and his elder brother and his wife to talk—not to mention the baby, whose diaper had to be changed.

Soon, Liang had to face another problem. He didn't have a girlfriend, even though he was reaching his thirties. It was no wonder, as it was out of the question for him to bring one home. He had tried only once, one winter evening. His family had evacuated long before the girl's arrival, and she seemed not to take immediate stock of the crammed room. They started talking about Dickens and Balzac while outside it drizzled. Time dripped away, like water from a broken gutter, as if lost in the nineteenth century. But there was no keeping his family out for too long. His grandfather, with a terrible cough, found himself outstaying his welcome in his neighbor's home. Then his elder brother, having finished half a pack of cigarettes outside in the midst of his wife's complaining, decided to bang on the door, albeit apologetically.

The girl did not come again, in spite of their common interests. After all, what's the point of dating and marrying a man without a room?

An old proverb says, no matter how clever and capable a woman, she cannot make dinner without rice. The same goes for a man. It was not Liang's fault, people in the lane agreed, that he still had no girlfriend.

At the beginning of the year, Liang learned that the institute would get an increased housing quota from the city government. It was what he had been long waiting for.

Before 1949, there were always rooms or apartments available for rent and sale to people who could afford them, but for many years after 1949, a government housing assignment system was in effect. In the name of socialist revolution, the system functioned through people's "work units"—factories, companies, hospitals, or institutes. Each work unit got its housing quota directly from the city authorities, and the ever-worsening city housing shortage created a burning issue for the work units, which were in charge of deciding which of their employees would get a room.

Housing was a crucial matter to Liang and his colleagues at the institute, which had a committee formed for the purpose. In the city of Shanghai, each and every person on the housing committee's waiting list had reasons why he or she deserved a room. It involved a lot of fact-checking and number-calculating for the committee to reach a decision. Liang put himself in the category of an "aged youth" on the application form to the housing committee: in the mid-eighties, an "aged youth" was a practical term used by the housing committee for those who remained single in their thirties. Liang argued that a room was the absolute precondition for marriage.

"Comrade Liang, there are three married couples waiting on the list. They still live together with their parents," the head of the housing committee said, implying Liang's case was not that urgent.

"But their housing conditions are not bad. Not bad at

all. Two couples have rooms for themselves, and the other one also has an attic. True, they still live with their parents, but that's not a problem." Liang argued passionately. "My case is totally different, with four generations under the ceiling of one single room."

"That's why you've also been pushed to the front of the waiting list, we all understand and we'll surely try our best for you, Comrade Liang."

But the competition became fiercer. Others on the waiting list also went running to the committee. It was true, as one argued, that Liang was still single, but it did not necessarily mean he already had a girlfriend, waiting to get married. In other words, his situation was not desperate, and he could still wait.

Out of frustration, Liang talked to others about the snag in the housing assignments. One of his sympathetic listeners was his friend Pingping, a bookseller. She was not a girlfriend; he had never thought of her that way. A fairly attractive girl, tall and slender, with almond-shaped eyes and cherry lips, Pingping was about his age.

"It's a catch-22. If you don't have a girlfriend, you won't get a room, but if you don't have a room, you can't get a girlfriend."

"Do you think you stand a good chance at your institute if you have a girlfriend?" she said.

"Yes, a very good chance, I think."

"Then go ahead and tell them I am your girlfriend."

"Oh," he said, surprised. He had never thought about it,

though he had heard stories about just such a "temporary girlfriend." He was touched by her generous offer. After all, the story of her dating him could easily get around, since his colleagues came to the bookstore a lot.

"Don't worry about it. People do these kind of things," she said emphatically, "a lot."

So he talked to the housing committee again, emphasizing the existence of his girlfriend.

"Come on, Liang. Now there is a girlfriend out of the blue? You've never talked about her before."

"But it's true. Her name is Pingping, she's a bookseller in the Xinhua bookstore on Nanjing Road. A lot of people at our institute go there regularly. That's why I have not talked to others about her. You may have already met her there too. We've known each other a long while."

"Pingping?" The head of the housing committee seemed incredulous. "Well, I can't simply take your word for it, can I? As people all say, to see is to believe."

Liang had no choice but to invite her to his office. She came, sat at his desk, and talked to him intimately for more than an hour. Afterward, they left together, hand in hand, telling people that they were going to dinner in Deda.

So they did. He felt obliged to, and the two sat at a table overlooking Nanjing Road, gradually lost in the ever-changing neon lights. The candlelight on the white, cloth-covered table lent a romantic atmosphere to the evening.

But the housing committee remained skeptical, and there

was a new response at Liang's next visit. "Her showing up at
your office doesn't really prove anything. There are stories
about girlfriends of convenience, you know. If you're ready
to marry, Liang, you'd better have a marriage certificate.
Something that shows proof of commitment. Otherwise,
people will say you brought her here simply to show her off."

Liang hesitated to break it to Pingping. What she had
done for him was incredibly generous and selfless, and it
would really be too much to ask her to make a marriage
commitment. A couple of days later, however, it was she
who raised the question at a café near the bookstore.

"How did it go at your housing committee?"

"They are suspicious. They think your visit does not
really prove anything."

"Really?" she said, looking him in the face.

He smiled an embarrassed smile without making any
further comment.

"I see. What would prove it?" she said with her head low.
"A marriage certificate, right? So show them the certificate.
It's just for the sake of the room. There would be no obliga-
tion, I mean, for you."

He stared at her, speechless. It might be not correct to
say that he liked her, but he surely did not dislike her. She
seemed able to constantly surprise him. At times, she appeared to be innocent, almost childlike, but at other times,
sophisticated, even calculating. She looked up at him, her
face radiant with a secret beauty flashing out from within.

"In for a penny," she said, "in for a pound."

In the dim light of the café, the choice seemed inevitable, her hand in his. The story about her being ready to marry him might have already started to spread anyway.

Later that afternoon, they went to the city civil administration office to get the marriage certificate.

Afterward, he went to the housing committee, holding the certificate, which had a red cover with the Chinese character of Double Happiness printed in gold on it.

"We believe you, Liang," the head of the committee said, pushing the certificate across the desk back to him, "but the others on the list have been married for years. One is expecting a baby late this year."

That evening, Pingping was waiting for him outside the institute, like a devoted new wife.

"So you have to play the last card," Pingping said after a pause in the gathering dusk, looking up at his office building, her head leaning on his shoulder. There was a black bat hovering around a half-open window, which he had forgotten to close after work. It was no big deal, since it was not his office alone.

"What last card?" he said in confusion, aware that the subtle perfume from her earlobe was making his mind wander.

"I've heard stories of a couple sleeping in the office—as an effective way of putting pressure on the housing committee."

"But how can I ask you to do that, Pingping?"

"There is a long sofa in your office, and I can sleep on that, I think. You'll take the desk with a bamboo mat spread out on it. That should work for the summer." She added thoughtfully, "We'll put a thermos bottle in the corner, and a basin too. Besides, there's the canteen on the first floor of your office building. We don't have anything to worry about."

He was flabbergasted by her observation. She had been to his office only once. It was too late, however, for him to say no. It would be too much a loss of face for him to back out at this stage. He hemmed and hawed, still hoping that she might not have really meant it. After all, it could also be too much a loss of face for her.

But true to her word, she came to his office the following afternoon with a traveling cart that carried thermos bottles, a washbasin, a spittoon, cups, a small alcohol stove, and, needless to say, new pillows and blankets and towels, which she must have just purchased.

His colleagues were too astonished to say anything, looking at one another like stupefied chickens. Embarrassed, they stood up in a hurry to get out of the office.

"No, you don't have to leave. I'm just leaving things here. And I won't come to join Liang until after your office hours in the evening. Sorry, we don't have any choice; for a married couple, you know, we have to have a room for ourselves."

She went on to pass small red envelopes of marriage candy to his colleagues, who all murmured congratulations. Liang actually got a red envelope too, which bore a large character of double happiness in shining gold, like the marriage certificate.

The candy he had picked out tasted as hard as a pebble, and it rolled around on his tongue for a long while without melting. Looking up, he noticed a black bat flickering about outside the window. Was it the same one he saw earlier when Pingping had told him about playing the last card?

When the evening fell, they were left alone in the office room.

It was a warm summer night. They found it hard to fall asleep, keenly aware that they were now married. The sofa was not long enough. She had to rest her bare feet on the sofa arm. The old desk was far more uncomfortable and groaned under his weight. They couldn't help gazing at each other in the dark. The occasional footsteps in the building had long since died out. It was getting hot in the office room with the windows closed and the door locked. She moved over to his desk, sat on the edge of it, and, without a word unbuttoned her blouse.

> Waves of the moonlight fading,
> A jade handle of the Dipper lowering,
> We calculate with our fingers
> When the west wind will come,
> Unaware of time flowing away like a river in the dark.

Afterward, they lay in silence with their legs entangled, pools of sweat on the hard desk on which he had worked since his first day as a research assistant at the institute. It was almost like a challenge to the system—a call to arms, he thought, remembering the title of a short story collection by Lu Xun, before losing himself in a dreamless blackness.

Early in the morning light, he opened his eyes to see Pingping moving about in her pajamas, pattering bare-foot in and out, carrying back a thermos bottle of hot water. Before he could wash himself with the new towel she handed to him, she was opening the door to greet his colleagues like a hostess, her laugh reverberating along the corridor like a silver bell.

He knew he didn't have to worry anymore about the housing assignment. He saw the conclusion in the eyes of his colleagues.

But he suddenly felt something like a chilly current surging down his spine that summer morning as he thought to himself, once again, that it was all for the sake of a room.

Still, it was a battle he had to win. He had to prove that he had the guts to fight to the end.

So the battle went on, triumphantly, to the end that she had predicted—he got the shining room key from the housing committee.

She was seven months pregnant by that time.

She decided not to move in immediately. It was an old room vacated by another family instead of a new room. But a room of twelve square meters nonetheless meant a new world to them. She wanted to renovate it like new. It was out of the question, however, for her to come to his office anymore. So he had her staying temporarily in Red Dust Lane, where his mother would help to take care of her. Only Pingping could be stubborn: she busied herself in and out of the lane, her feet swollen and her face pale, supervising the renovation project, choosing and bargaining for the most inexpensive yet excellent material.

Liang still slept in the office. He was getting used to it. He did not have to worry about the morning traffic, and he worked quite late at night, though no one knew exactly what he had been doing there.

But there was another reason for staying at the office. He didn't want to witness the constant bickering between Pingping and his mother, who believed that the younger woman had tricked him into marriage. After all, Pingping was several months older than he, another "aged female youth," and it might have been her last chance to hook such a deal. He was inclined to agree with his mother, thinking about all the initiatives Pingping had taken, though he didn't say anything to his pregnant wife. From the moment he had first raised the subject of housing, Pingping had never let him drop it—despite all her casual remarks and seeming lack of concern for herself.

He also had no answer to his mother's question, "What do you see in her?"

That is, except the room that came with her. But it had been her room in all honesty, because it came to him through her effort and her sacrifice. He could not help wondering at the sight of this bloated woman, almost a stranger, nagging and bickering in the lane where he had grown up. There was hardly any trace of vivaciousness left in her, he observed with a twinge of conscience as she handed him a white towel, her face dust-covered and her hair disheveled from her renovation project.

One night, waking up alone in the dark office, he shivered at the prospect of his married life in that room of twelve square feet, year after year, with his wife, his children, and perhaps his grandchildren too, all growing up under the same roof, just like in Red Dust Lane. There was no possibility of having a second room assigned to him by the institute.

And his wife had not talked to him about his work at the institute for months, or about Balzac or Dickens, or such writers as she used to discuss with him in the bookstore. She's too busy, he thought, an interpretation he tried to adhere to. And he didn't bother to explain to her what he had been busy with, working late at the institute.

He almost missed the expected date of his son's birth.

At the "first month celebration dinner" held for his son in the lane, he turned over his room key to his wife, declaring that he was going to start his own business in Shenzhen. It was a special economic zone, where with the new government policies, people could do things that were not yet possible in other parts of socialist China. There, people were capable of making more money as entrepreneurs and buying new apartments for themselves. He had made an intensive study of it and had come up with a business plan.

"China is going to change," he said simply. "I'm planning to buy a new apartment there for ourselves."

Iron Rice Bowl

(1990)

This is the last issue of *Red Dust Lane Blackboard Newsletter* for the year 1990. China successfully weathered the political storm of 1989. Martial law was lifted in Beijing. Hundreds of arrested student-movement participants, having confessed, were released. In April, the Basic Law of the Hong Kong Special Administrative Region of the PRC was adopted to ensure a fifty-year continuance of Hong Kong's economic system.

In the ongoing economic reform, the process of restructuring or closing state-owned enterprises was accelerated. The year also witnessed the rapid modernization of the People's Liberation Army. "A clear sky after the rain," we are full of confidence for the future of the socialist China.

Dong Keqiang had always been considered one of the luckiest young men in Red Dust Lane. Since his grandfather's generation, the Dongs had lived here, with a whole wing in a *shikumen* house for themselves. Unlike others in the lane, his grandfather, a skilled, well-paid technician before 1949, was capable of renting a wing consisting of a dining room, a living room, a bedroom, and a small dark room, which served as a bathroom. In the years afterward, those rooms gradually lost their original function as the family grew and the rooms had to accommodate more and more people. Still, Dong had a room all to himself, and as the only male heir, he would eventually inherit the wing.

But his luck was more than just the wing. After 1949, his grandfather was classified in the new socialist class system as a worker, and so was his father. In the seventies, when Dong grew up, a proletarian family background still meant a lot. Dong himself became a Little Red Guard, a member of the Communist Youth League, and in time, a technician at Shanghai Telecommunication, a well-paid position at a profitable state-run company—an iron rice bowl.

"An iron rice bowl" was a figure of speech that evolved from the time-honored tradition of eating rice from a bowl. When someone lost his job, it was often said that he lost or broke his rice bowl. In the state-run enterprise system established after 1949, employees never got laid off—no matter their work performance—but instead held their jobs until they retired with a pension and medical insurance. These were the benefits of the socialist system.

So a job at a state-run company was called an "iron rice bowl" because job security was absolute—an iron rice bowl would never break in the equalitarianist system.

In the economic reform in the mid-eighties, when some people began to run their own businesses, "iron rice bowl holders" didn't take it as something to worry about. The possibility that those new "entrepreneurs" might earn a little more would be nothing compared to all the benefits of an iron rice bowl. Besides, no one could tell how those new things would work out in China.

One afternoon, Auntie Jia, the celebrated matchmaker of Red Dust Lane, introduced Dong to Lili, a fashionable young girl. Lili had been reluctant to meet an ordinary technician, but Auntie Jia made a convincing point about Dong's grandfather being in his eighties and about Dong inheriting the whole wing in the near future.

Dong and Lili met at Bund Park, and Dong was smitten at first sight. They talked and laughed and walked in the park for a couple of hours. He then suggested they go to dinner at a restaurant that same evening. Looking across the street, she suggested a restaurant in the Peace Hotel, a five-star hotel he had never stepped in before, but he didn't hesitate. He had enough money with him, he believed, for the evening.

So they went up to the restaurant on the seventh floor and chose a table by the window overlooking the river. Instead of looking at the river, though, he kept gazing into the waves in her large eyes, which he imagined set the colorful vessels sailing along the river below them. She said she liked the atmosphere here.

But he was shocked at the prices in the gold-printed menu. It was out of the question for him to try and impress her by choosing one of the expensive chef's specials. So without turning over the menu to her, he started ordering like a pro: "Pork with Tree Ears, Imperial Concubine Chicken, Meat Ball of Four Happiness, Single Winter Bamboo Shoot Soup . . ." Each of the dishes he ordered cost less than a hundred yuan. Lili didn't say anything; instead she kept looking out of the window, absentmindedly.

"What about fish and shrimp?" the waitress said, casting a casual glance at the menu in his hand.

It was a question he had dreaded. An Australian lobster served three ways—raw slices, stir-fried with scallion and ginger, and watery rice of the lobster sauce—cost nine hundred yuan. He didn't even bother to check the price for a large croaker fried in the shape of a squirrel. Not that he was tight-fisted, but he had only about eight hundred yuan with him. He glanced through the menu again. To his relief, he found something listed in the chef's specials: "Live Yellow River Carp."

The carp was not considered, to the best of his knowledge, an expensive delicacy. In the food market at the back of the lane, a kilo of carp was no more than three or four yuan. A live carp could cost slightly more, but not that much. The chef's special was marked with something called "unit price": sixteen yuan. Whether "unit" meant kilo or *jing*—a standard Chinese measurement equivalent to half a kilo—the price appeared acceptable.

"How about a carp about one to one and a half kilos?" the waitress suggested considerately, following his focus on the menu. "Anything smaller won't have much meat, but a larger one won't be tender."

"That sounds perfect."

Lili turned to him with spring waves rippling in her eyes—possibly rippling with the swimming carp.

Soon their orders appeared on the table. In spite of all the delicacies, he feasted his eyes only on her. She started eating, dabbing at her lush lips with a pink napkin, smiling radiantly in the miraculous late sunshine streaming through the window.

Then the live carp was served by another waitress, who was dressed in an indigo wax print, her bare feet in wooden slippers, and her shapely ankles silver-bangled, lighting up the red carpet. She placed before them the carp on a huge willow-patterned platter, saying with a dramatic flare, "Look!"

The eyes of the fish on the platter were still turning. How the fish was cooked, he had no idea, but it was nothing short of a miracle. Lili chopsticked a slice of back meat onto his plate. It tasted extraordinary—delicious and fresh—and even more so with her intimate gesture. She sucked at the tender fish cheek with a sensual grace beyond his wildest dream, her slender fingers lightly touching her lips.

Suddenly clumsy and jumpy, he plucked out one eye of the carp with the chopstick, splashing up the juice.

"The meat surrounding the eye is the best," she said with a reassuring smile. "In Hong Kong, there's a special dish of fish eyes. Only eight orders per day."

The meat surrounding the carp eye tasted like fat tofu with a nondescript texture. He had never heard about the Hong Kong special dish. She might be a regular customer in fancy restaurants, he concluded. But she deserved it, because, as a proverb says, a smile on her lips was worth a thousand tons of gold.

He wasn't aware of time flowing away like the river in the gathering dusk.

She finally sighed with content. The waitress came over to their table with the bill on a silver tray.

It was a big shock—the bill was more than 2,500 yuan. He had done the calculation in his mind several times. The amount shouldn't exceed six hundred, with his fish weighing about a kilo. So he summoned the waitress and asked her about it.

"Oh, the unit price means a *liang*, equivalent to fifty grams."

"How can that possibly be?"

"It's a convention in five-star restaurants. You've never been to one before?"

"Of course I have."

"Then you should have known about the unit price,"

she said, turning to the last page of the menu. "Take a look. It states it clearly."

It was true—it was printed in tiny characters there, though he had never thought to check at the end of the menu. If he weren't in Lili's company, he might have admitted his ignorance, paid with whatever money he had with him, and then paid the remaining balance later. But he couldn't afford to lose face like that. As an alternative, he tried to come off as a man fighting for principle, not for money. Only this way, he thought, would he stand a chance in her eyes, though it was difficult for him to define the principle or the fight for it.

"Come on. The Shanghai newspapers are filled with stories about rip-offs like this," he said. "My buddy works for the *Wenhui Daily*. He would jump on a story like this."

"What would the article possibly say?" the waitress asked sarcastically.

"It's no longer the days of Victor Sassoon," Dong said, invoking the name of the Jewish tycoon who built the Peace Hotel with money exploited from Chinese people. "The fish costs more than two months of my salary as a state-run company worker. Do you think that's socialist?"

"So you are still holding onto an iron rice bowl," she said. "You know what? The customers here are holding gold bowls and silver bowls. They have their own companies. Let me tell you—we are not a state-run restaurant. If you are so proud of your iron bowl, you don't have to come here."

While he was arguing with the waitress, Lili stood up and left the table without a word. She might have gone to the restroom, he thought.

But she didn't come back.

Then restaurant security came, took all the money he had, and dragged him out by the collar.

Afterward, when he tried to contact Lili again, she said on the phone, "Perhaps you can afford to lose face like that, but I can't."

Dong couldn't afford to lose face like that either. So he quit his state-run company and left for Shenzhen with a business plan of his own.

There he started manufacturing stainless-steel rice bowls, believing that the archetype of the iron rice bowl still held symbolic significance for people. It proved to be a brilliant idea, and they soon began selling all over the country.

Return of POW II

(1992)

This is the last issue of *Red Dust Lane Newsletter* for the year 1992. In January, Comrade Deng Xiaoping made his strategic "southern tour" to Shenzhen and Zhuhai Special Economic Zones, pointing out that revolution is the liberation of production forces, that reform is also the liberation of production forces, and that development, instead of being either socialist or capitalist, is the one and only truth. His important talk gave a great boost to the open-door economic strategies and accelerated the market reform to establish a socialist market economy, with major Yangtze River and border cities opening to foreign investment. Internationally, China ratified the Nuclear Non-Proliferation Treaty. And this year, China's GDP grew by twelve percent.

Bai Jie's story should have finished long, long ago.

It almost did, in 1954, the year she returned to Red Dust Lane after being taken and released as a POW of the Korean War. Since then, she had led a quiet but hardly visible life in the lane.

Her existence wasn't written off, even though she was merely a shadow of her former self. What happened to her in the years after was of barely any interest to anybody in the lane. Still, she didn't live in a vacuum. Whenever there was a new political movement, suspicions about her would come up again. And there were a number of new political movements during those years. It seemed quite possible that at some point the suspicions would bear fruit, but they never did.

Those years were like short sentences punctuated by one political movement after another, and one individual's story—not particularly tragic or dramatic in comparison to many others—couldn't hold people's attention for long. She had been brought up again only once in the evening talk of the lane. It was at the beginning of the Cultural Revolution: a radical young Red Guard branded the Chinese character "Loyalty" on her own shoulder to show her devotion to Mao, and someone brought up the topic of Bai.

"What people put her through is a shame," Old Root snapped. "Don't even mention her again."

A lot had happened to the people who knew her story back in the early fifties. Some moved, some died, and some simply lost interest. The young and the middle-aged people who joined the evening talk of the lane weren't very interested in a withered, white-haired woman.

The water flows, flowers fall, and the spring fades. / It's a changed world.

Bai had retired from the hospital a couple of years ago. Still single, she stayed at home—in her room of eleven square feet—most of the time. She had bought a hot plate, so instead of mixing with her neighbors in the common kitchen, she also cooked in her own room. Even the people who lived in the same building saw little of her. One of her next-door neighbors thought Bai might have some sort of mental disorder. Or she simply wanted to pass into oblivion.

She might have succeeded, but for the unexpected return of Xue Zhiming, another prisoner of war, who appeared about forty years later, in 1992. His was a totally different story.

Xue had been another of the Chinese People's Volunteers marching proudly out of Red Dust Lane, leaving for the Korean War. A gawky young man, he was by no means as popular as Bai, and the lane paid little attention to the news about him being listed as having disappeared during the Korean War. Later on, there was some speculation about him being captured. Shortly after Bai's return, a police officer visited his parents too. Their talk was behind closed doors, and no one ever learned the contents. No red paper flower ever appeared on the door, and even his parents hardly talked about him in the lane. When they passed away in the early seventies, there was no further news of Xue. It was believed that he must have died.

It was not until the early nineties that a different story began to come out. Xue was alive—and prosperous, too—in Taiwan. As it turned out, he had been captured in the same battle as Bai and put into the same prison camp, but instead of returning home when released, he went over to Taiwan, where he was given a considerable sum from the Nationalist regime in exchange for his denouncement of the Communist regime. There, he started his own business and succeeded. By the early nineties, he was a billionaire with several large companies to his name. There was no news of him in Red Dust Lane for many years, and he didn't contact home for fear of bringing punishment or trouble down on the people.

With the dramatic change in the political environment across the Taiwan strait, Xue thought about coming back for a visit. He approached the Shanghai city government, inquiring about the possibility and expressing his wish to do something for his home city. His request was instantly granted. It was no longer the time of Chairman Mao's class struggle. China had now opened up to the world, and particularly to foreign capital coming in from anywhere. Besides, people now had some access to events in the outside world. For one thing, they read stories about Mitterrand, the French president who had been captured by the Ger-

mans during the Second World War, an experience that
hadn't cast a shadow over his political life. As for Xue's
decision to go to Taiwan, it was easily brushed aside as
a matter of history. According to a popular Party slogan,
people should look forward, not backward.

The city government wanted the neighborhood committee of Red Dust Lane to do a good job welcoming Xue
home. It was a political assignment, as it was an opportunity for the city to acquire outside investment capital, and
it would help to propagandize the "new united front" as
well. Xue was said to have a special attachment to the lane.
Comrade Jun, the head of the neighborhood committee,
ordered a clean-and-dress-up for the whole neighborhood.
Several lane representatives were selected, including those
old-timers who had known Xue before the Korean War.

When Xue arrived in Shanghai, as expected, he signed
an intention agreement with the local government about
a joint venture in the Huangpu district that could potentially add at least two hundred jobs to the area. He also
gave a large donation to the elementary school he had attended, and in return, the school renamed the library the
Zhiming Library.

The climax of Xue's visit was going to take place during his visit to Red Dust Lane. He carried a large number
of red envelopes in his briefcase, it was said, for the people
in the lane.

The neighborhood committee suggested a "wind-
receiving" banquet for Xue in Xinya Restaurant, but Xue

insisted on choosing a small restaurant on Fujian Road, close to the side entrance of the lane. It wasn't too surprising. He must have had enough of dining in five-star restaurants.

"It's the lane in my dreams," Xue said, the wine rippling in his cup.

"In your dreams, it's not just the lane, but the whole mainland too," Comrade Jun said, raising his cup high. "We are all proud of you, Mr. Xue."

"It's nothing—it's just like the old Chinese saying," Xue said. "In the end, a leaf falls back down to the tree's root."

"To Red Dust Lane," the people of the lane affirmed, raising their cups around the table, their many arms like a forest.

After the first few rounds of toasts, Xue asked, "How is Bai Jie?"

It was understandable that he was concerned, while in his cups, about a fellow POW, as he sat in a restaurant so close to the lane. Long, long ago, he might even have been one of her secret admirers.

The lane representatives didn't know how to answer him, looking at each other in embarrassment. Comrade Jun mumbled that Bai was sick, which was true. According to the latest information from her neighbors, she might even have early Alzheimer's.

Holding a piece of stewed bear paw with his chopsticks, Xue continued, emotionally, "For many years, I have thought of her constantly. What has happened to her, back in Red Dust Lane?"

What had really happened to Bai? For all these years, she had lived in the lane, single, solitary, like a hermit crab forever staying within a borrowed shell, as all the political trouble loomed over her. Comrade Jun came up with the excuse that he didn't start to work in the lane until the sixties, so he didn't exactly know. Old Root, on the other hand, suggested that Xue start by telling them about what had happened to him during the years since he left.

Draining the cup, Xue started to tell us about his experiences during the Korean War.

He and Bai had been put in the same prison camp, where the Taiwanese agents tried hard to talk them into defecting to Taiwan. At first Xue was quite adamant in his refusal. What finally brought him around was a story told by one of the agents, whose uncle, a nuclear scientist at an American university, went back to mainland China, but couldn't find a job in his field because no one trusted him. In the class system of socialist China, Xue's father was a "small business owner," and he wasn't trusted in the new society either. It wasn't difficult for Xue to conclude that, even if he returned to Red Dust Lane, he would always be under suspicion, and he dreaded such a prospect. The compensation offered by the Nationalist regime was, needless to say, another factor that influenced his decision. It was an amount equal to his total income for twenty years back at the snack shop he had worked in.

"Right or wrong, it was a decision that weighed like a rock on my heart whenever I thought of her," Xue said. "She was a young girl, but she had the guts to stand up for her principles. She said no to all the offers and ignored all the threats so that she could come back."

"Don't be so hard on yourself, Mr. Xue," Comrade Jun said. "It was long ago and things were complicated in those days. It wasn't exactly your fault. History has turned over a new page and you have come back to the lane."

"We heard stories about the prison camps, stories of torture or branding of prisoners," Old Root cut in unexpectedly. "Was that true?"

"It's possible, especially with Bai, who refused to cooperate at all with Taiwanese agents. As for branding, we heard stories of it in the camp too," Xue said. He massaged his brows as if in pain before he went on. "They threatened to brand anticommunist slogans on us, I heard, so that it would be impossible for us to come back. To forestall such a dirty trick, Bai used a burning needle to engrave 'Long Live Chairman Mao!' on her left shoulder."

"Oh, she could have showed it to the Party authorities—" Comrade Jun cut himself short after a glance from Old Root.

"I really admire her," Xue said, his head low. "She never wavered. There was a wealthy Taiwanese officer who was mad for her. He later became a general and if she had consented . . ."

It was obvious that Xue was still waiting for his old

neighbors to tell him more about Bai, but they chose not to. No point dampening his spirits with a sad story, particularly as Bai might even have been the reason why he had left for the Korean War, as well as the reason he had come back after all these years. Knowledge that he had made the right decision—that if he had come back in the fifties, he would have ended up just like Bai, or even worse— might have given him some comfort, but it would be cold comfort.

Finally, the host and the guests all got drunk.

That night, Bai shut herself up in the small room, mumbling as always to the faded portrait of Mao on the wall. She never heard a word of what Xue said over at the banquet. Nor, if the rumor about her Alzheimer's was true, would she have understood.

Old Hunchback Fang

(1995)

This is the last issue of *Red Dust Lane Blackboard Newsletter* for the year 1995. Early this year, China tested missiles and held military exercises in the Taiwan Strait, showing its unwavering determination to fight for the unification of the country. New educational legislation now stipulates nine years of compulsory education. In September, the Central Party Committee adopted the proposition to further the economic reform through the transformation of the traditional state-planned economy to a socialist market economy. Our government took effective measures to curb inflation, which had reached seventeen percent.

Let me make this point first, my old neighbors in Red Dust Lane. A story is never really independent of the storyteller. Say what you may, but someone has made the choice to tell this story, not that story. Why? Simply because this narrative has a specific meaning for the narrator. For instance, I'm going to talk about Old Hunchback Fang this evening. It has a lot to do with what has happened to me—directly or not that directly—through all the years. More than twenty years, to be exact.

My second point: a story doesn't come out of the blue, nor does it have a certain closure. Between Old Hunchback Fang and me, a real face-to-face encounter didn't occur until this week, though things far more important to him, and to me—a lot of them related and interrelated—had happened years earlier.

Now, I am not prejudiced against a man with deformities. My father was also crippled—during the Cultural Revolution. I simply don't know Fang's full name. As far as I remember, everybody here has always called him by that particular nickname. So did Fang himself. You object to it? Fine, I'll call him Fang. If I have a slip of the tongue, it's just because his hunchback seems to have special meaning, a symbolic correspondence to what I'm going to say.

I first heard of Fang in the early sixties, when he was a worker just retired from the Shanghai No. 3 Textile Mill, and an honorable member of the neighborhood committee. An old man, short, bald, wearing a pair of old-fashioned glasses that looked like the bottoms of beer bottles, and with a hunchback like an upturned iron wok. The neighborhood committee seemed irrelevant to me as a kid. I simply saw it as an office for housewives to make petty family complaints or receive food ration coupons.

The outbreak of the Cultural Revolution changed everything. The committee was now focused on mobilizing the people to "battle and campaign against the class enemies." As Mao said, "We have to push the continuous revolution under the proletarian dictatorship to the end." It pushed Fang to the fore, who gave a passionate speech about "Savoring the Present Sweetness and Recalling the Past Bitterness" at a neighborhood meeting.

"What am I? A poor, pathetic hunchback. In the old society before 1949, I was looked down upon like trash. One day I slipped and fell in front of the lane, and several young hooligans came over and began kicking, spitting on me, and cursing, 'What an old turtle has turned over.' Comrades, it's only under the socialist system that I began to lead a happy, wonderful life. Because of my deformity, I was allowed to retire at the age of forty-five with a full pension. Could I have ever dreamed of it before the liberation in 1949? No, no way. I owe everything to the Party, to Chairman Mao. Whoever dares to be against Chairman Mao, I will fight him to my last breath in the latest direction of the class struggle."

The speech was sincere, but too short. The example given was not that well-chosen, either. There are hooligans in the past and in the present, and it wasn't the old society that caused Fang to be derided. As for the "latest direction of the class struggle," Fang could hardly understand the ever-changing political terms in the newspapers—he simply recorded and repeated them like a machine.

Shortly afterward, a neighborhood group was formed and named the Mao Zedong Thought Propaganda Team, which consisted of a dozen retirees, a gigantic drum, several brass gongs and cymbals, and a pile of colorful paper posters. Fang held a bullhorn in one hand, clutching in his other a list of class enemies. With his red armband shining like an enflamed cloud in the morning, he led the team marching to the targeted houses of class enemies throughout the lane.

In front of the first targeted house, his bullhorn would start booming: "Down with capitalist roader Zhang Shan. We must trample him underfoot thousands of times, so that he can't turn over for the next hundred years." Then at the next door: "Down with counterrevolutionary Li Si. For your antisocialism crime, you deserve to die thousands of times." And then at the third door: "Down with rightist Huang Huizhong, you have to confess your crime to the people."

Fang had a loud voice, which had a metallic quality as a result of his malformed lung capacity. His eyes glared knives, his nostrils issued forth fire. For a split second, he loomed gigantic—the proletarian wrath incarnated.

The revolutionary activities of the team were supposed to bring pressure against the class enemies. There was a popular slogan at the time: "The proletarian dictatorship

must be carried into every corner of our socialist society."
Into every corner of Red Dust Lane, too.

Consequently, Fang's path and mine crossed for the first
time. My father was a middle-ranking Party cadre who
suddenly became a "capitalist roader" in 1966. Hence a class
enemy too. Fang arrived dutifully at our door with his
bullhorn: "Burn the stinking capitalist roader! Fry the rotten capitalist roader! Scalp the damned capitalist roader!"

The revolutionary mass-criticism increased in its inten-
sity. Soon the class enemies were marched onto a make-
shift stage, bearing huge blackboards around their necks
with their names written on them and crossed out. Old
Hunchback Fang proved to be the most active, and creative
too, in producing those blackboards, as if he had an inex-
haustible supply of energy from his hunchback. The sight
of him struck a new terror into the hearts of the people on
the list clutched in his hand.

"Don't cry," a young mother would hush her baby in
the cradle, "or Old Hunchback Fang will come." It was
an apt adaptation from an old Chinese saying: *Don't cry, or
the white-eyed wolf will come.*

I was young, yet not too young to tremble in my father's shoes. It seemed to be a matter of time before he
would step onto a mass-criticism stage, standing with a
blackboard dangling around his neck. What was worse,
his left leg was broken during a mass-criticism meeting at
his factory, and during a similar neighborhood meeting
I might have to support him like a crutch, standing with

him on the stage. The image of me as a human crutch gave me continuous nightmares. One night, I was jolted out of bed by Fang's voice thundering across the lane. "Capitalist roader Guohua, you are doomed!" Rubbing my sleepy eyes, I rushed downstairs, only to find no one there. I had heard his voice, I swore, but the neighborhood kids might have imitated it as a practical joke, as my father said, or I could have dreamed of it.

Fortunately, I didn't have to become such a crutch for my father in a public humiliation. He was suddenly liberated from his "capitalist roader" status by another Red Guard organization which, in a surprising bid for power, declared my father an "educable revolutionary cadre" on their side.

Little did I expect that Fang would come to cast a more direct shadow. In 1969, Mao launched forth the movement of sending educated youths to the countryside. In response, millions and millions of middle and high school graduates left home to "receive reeducation from the poor and lower-middle-class peasants." A few were left behind, including me: I was a "waiting-for-assignment youth" left in the city, excused due to bronchitis.

The Mao Zedong Thought Propaganda Team shifted focus to the new targets of the Cultural Revolution: the educated youths that remained in the city. Fang and his followers applied the same tactics of public humiliation and pressure with different slogans. "As our great leader Chairman Mao teaches us, it is necessary for the educated youths to go to the countryside to receive reeducation from the poor and lower-middle-class peasants." It was a long sentence, but Fang's loud voice jumped out against a deafening clangor of gongs and drums. It worked like a formula. While marching from one house to another, he went through the names on his list. "Zhou Wu, you don't listen to Chairman Mao. You must be responsible for the consequences!" "Chen Liu, you are against the movement of educated youths. You have to mend your ways!"

There were actually two educated youths, Zhengming and I, in the same *shikumen* house. The only difference between us was that he didn't have an excuse like bronchitis. So I was spared for the moment, but his name came loud and clear out of Fang's bullhorn. "You have to go now, Zhengming, or, day and night, we will never give you a break."

Fang and his followers made their rounds three times a day: in the early morning, in the afternoon, and in the late evening, so that the maximum number of people could hear their message. It was an effective tactic, bringing not only pressure to the educated youths in the list but also annoyance to the neighbors, who couldn't complain about the propaganda but could only vent their frustration against the young people.

"You'd better go, Zhengming," Granny Hua said to him in the common kitchen of our *shikumen* building, "or we will never have peace here."

Zhengming consulted with me. He felt so guilty that

he was ready to give in to the continuous nerve-wracking pressure. I didn't offer him any advice. My father was sick with rheumatism, and I couldn't afford to bring any additional problems home.

"The moment my name comes out of Fang's bullhorn," I said lamely, "I may have to leave too."

So Zhengming left. In less than a year, he had lost three fingers in a tractor accident. It was said that he did it on purpose, so he would be able to return to the city—in accordance with a government policy concerning a handicapped educated youth. I knew little about it. I was too worried for myself. At the familiar sound of the drums and gongs, I would jump up and peek out from behind the curtain, trembling. The Mao Zedong Thought Propaganda Team was planning to find new targets among the educated youths left behind, and bronchitis wasn't considered as good an excuse anymore.

Again, as luck would have it, before my name came out of Fang's bullhorn, the movement of educated youths came to an abrupt halt. Instead of transforming themselves into poor and lower-middle-class peasants in the countryside, most of the young people failed to keep the pot boiling in those faraway villages. Mao himself wrote a letter, admitting that there might be some problems with the movement.

But Fang's team had already started on another campaign. From my window, I could hear Fang shouting new slogans. During those years, there were so many political campaigns, Fang didn't have to worry.

After the end of the Cultural Revolution, I went to college in Beijing. To my surprise, in the midst of my studies there, I found myself thinking of Old Hunchback Fang quite a few times. According to my father, Fang started working for the neighborhood security committee after the dissolution of the Mao Zedong Thought Propaganda Team. He was still patrolling the neighborhood market as a sort of watchdog, still wearing a red armband—though a different one, of course.

I didn't have a clear picture of Fang's new revolutionary activity until I came back to Shanghai in the early eighties and began working as a journalist for the *Wenhui Daily* newspaper. In those days, the Party authorities had already started the economic reform in Shenzhen, but in Shanghai and other large cities, the presence of private peddlers at a state-run neighborhood market was still considered a threat in the eyes of the orthodox. So Fang's job consisted of forcibly confiscating the peddlers' bamboo baskets and stomping on them vigorously. He must have derived a big kick from it, imagining himself as a staunch pillar of socialism whenever he drove away a weeping country wench.

It wasn't too much of a surprise to see Old Hunchback Fang looming in the market, patrolling energetically as if with steel springs under his feet, but I was surprised at the ferocity he showed toward those peddlers. After all, they were not class enemies, not like in the old days, and I happened to notice that the Party newspapers were talking about the coexistence of different ownerships in China's new economy.

"That old bastard's out of his mind," Zhengming cursed, binding a live river crab he had just bought from a private vendor.

I didn't have a personal grudge against Fang. What prompted me to confront him was another stroke of misplaced yin and yang. I had no idea at all—not at the time—that it would come to influence both of our lives, though in different ways.

Now in those days, my job in the *Wenhui* office kept me quite busy. One Saturday afternoon, I hurried back to the lane to make dinner for my father. In the nearby food market, I saw a middle-aged woman preparing a bucket of rice-paddy eels by a public sink. What caught my attention, I could not tell, but I found myself slowing to a halt and watching. She was whipping an eel against the concrete curb, fixing its head on a thick nail at the end of a wooden bench, drawing the eel tight, cutting through its belly, pulling out its bones and insides, chopping off its head, and slicing its body delicately. Her hands and arms were covered in eel blood, and her bare feet too. She made a few pennies by selling the bones and entrails to restaurants, which used them to make special noodle soups.

Then recognition came. She was Qing, the "queen" in my high school, who left for the countryside with the first group of educated youths in 1970. I had heard stories of her tragic life in the countryside. Now a single mother with a kid, she looked at least fifteen years older than her real age. The chopped-off heads of the eels were scattered at her feet, about the size of her bare toes, their eyes still staring. She didn't recognize me.

On an impulse, I decided to buy a kilo of live eels to make a Shanghai-flavored dish of fried eel slices for my father. I was reaching for my wallet when a commotion broke out in the market. Old Hunchback Fang was rushing over, surprisingly swift like a hawk, and he clutched Qing's collar. I was too startled to react, catching only a glimpse of her being dragged away in the direction of the neighborhood committee.

Then I became furious. For all these years, he had been like a curse. First to my father, then to me, now to her. But she was so pitiable, an ex–educated youth, jobless and skill-less, with a family relying on her eel-blood-covered hands. She did not really sell anything of her own in the market. How much could she possibly earn for those eel bones?

So I decided to do something. That night I gathered together a bunch of the latest Party documents regarding the reform of the socialist ownership system. After having made a thorough study of them, I had a long talk with Comrade Jun, the head of the neighborhood committee.

"It's no longer an era when people put the issue of class struggle above everything," I pointed out to him. "According to the *People's Daily*, such an overemphasis is not helpful to the reform. The times have changed, and a free, private market has become a necessary supplement to the socialist state market. It's wrong for Fang to treat the peddlers like that."

Comrade Jun kept nodding throughout my lecture, without attempting to interrupt.

"So you have to take away his red armband, I'm afraid," I concluded. "People could say or write something about it. That might do a lot of harm to the image of Red Dust Lane."

It must have sounded like a serious threat to Comrade Jun, who promised to do something about it.

Sure enough, there was no sign of Fang patrolling around during my next visit to the market. It was said that he trembled like a fallen leaf when he was turning over his red armband. I didn't see Qing there, either. That might have been just as well. My memory of her seemed to have been sullied by the eel blood.

In the developing economic reform, I saw an opportunity to start my own business. Actually, I first got the idea when studying the documents that night to drive Fang out of the market. So I left Shanghai for Guangzhou, and then Guangzhou for Hong Kong. What happened afterward was, to put it simply, one business deal after another. Suffice it to say that I have been quite lucky so far.

A business trip brought me back to Shanghai a few days ago. So much had changed in the neighborhood of Red Dust Lane that I could hardly believe my eyes.

A number of snack booths had mushroomed up here. Close to the entrance of the lane, there was also a lunch-box booth consisting of two or three wooden tables, seven or eight benches, and a big coal-burning stove in an open kitchen. It was convenient to the residents of the lane, and to the employees of nearby companies too.

I was shocked to see Old Hunchback Fang there. He looked different—though not surprisingly so—from what I remembered from the days of his bullhorn and red arm-band. He had shrunken into himself, become almost a dwarf, and his hunchback was even more pronounced. His head hung low, cutting almost a ninety degree angle to the bottom of his spine. What flabbergasted me, however, was that he was working as a busboy there, having to stand on tiptoe to reach the plates on the high shelf.

I sat down at a table and ordered a bowl of noodles with fried pork and pickles. He came over. Believe it or not, it was the first actual face-to-face encounter between us—his face at the same level as mine. The old man didn't recognize me as I took the bowl from the tray that he was holding head-high.

It was a privately run snack place, something he had so long fought against. The owner of the lunch booth turned out to be no other than Zhengming. I asked him to sit with me.

According to Zhengming, the economic reform had hit several pensioners in the lane hard. In the past, whether a state-run company was profitable or not, retirees had always received the pension and medical benefits from the state. Now it was up to the company itself, and Fang's state-run textile mill had fallen into terrible shape. He couldn't get even half of his original pension. With rising inflation, it was common for retired people to have to find a second job after retirement.

"He had a little extra income when he was working with the neighborhood committee," Zhengming said, "but several years ago, he was fired for some reason. I took pity on him and I pay him two hundred yuan a month, in addition to free meals."

I didn't tell Zhengming that I was the reason for Fang's dismissal from the neighborhood committee. From a different perspective, it was another stroke of irony: Fang might have been the catalyst for my venture into the business world.

I looked around. No one was leaving tips. Tipping was still "politically incorrect" in socialist China. Still, I left a ten yuan bill on the table when I left.

(Tofu) Worker Poet Bao II

(1996)

This is the last issue of *Red Dust Lane Blackboard Newsletter* for the year 1996. It was another great year in China's unprecedented economic and social reform. China, Russia, Kazakhstan, Kyrgyzstan, and Tajikistan held a landmark summit in Shanghai. The so-called Shanghai Five all agreed to reduce military forces along their shared borders. In the economic front, China successfully reduced inflation to six percent, while its GDP grew ten percent.

Worker Poet Bao's Tofu—that small tofu booth of his standing in front of Red Dust Lane was more than a nine-day wonder.

The new businesses in the nineties generally had one thing in common: their short life. According to statistics in the *People's Daily*, several hundred companies went out of business every day. Now, the tofu booth in question barely qualified as a business entity, since it consisted of a small stone mill to grind soybeans, a couple of wooden pails, and a shelf on which the tofu products for sale were displayed. But the business had lasted for months and showed no sign of faltering.

At his booth, Bao developed and displayed a colorful array of homemade soybean products—white tofu, soft and hard tofu, frozen tofu for hot pot, golden tofu skin, gray tofu dredges, milky soybean drink, brown vegetable chicken, yellow fried gluten—all of which were far more delicious than those sold in the state-run market. In the afternoon, Bao also started selling stinking tofu, which was fried in a wok over a tiny stove. A stick of three golden pieces with a lot of red pepper sauce over them sold for only twenty cents. Soon it wasn't only customers from the lane who flocked to the booth, as its reputation spread.

According to Bao, he had learned a number of secret recipes from that Ningbo tofu shop back in the fifties, prior to his arrival in Shanghai. That made his tofu really different. However, there was another reason for the extraordinarily brisk business. As it was pointed out in a local newspaper, some of the customers came out of curiosity to see how a famous worker poet came to sell tofu. It was a metamorphosis beyond their imagining.

"They would never be able to understand the real story," Four-Eyed Liu observed during the evening talk of the lane, holding a paper bowl of almond tofu in his hand. "Only the people in the lane have witnessed the gradual change. Alas, Bao would never be able sell his poetry like he does tofu. He's still a member of the Writers' Association, isn't he?"

"As Lao-tzu says, fortune begets misfortune. There's no telling how things come around in this world—starting from a small piece of tofu," Old Root said, tapping his fingers meditatively on the edge of the bamboo chair. It was a sign that there would be another intriguing story told from his special perspective, and several young audience members gathered around. "Like so many stories in China, the story can be traced back to the Cultural Revolution."

The Cultural Revolution affected Bao like it did everybody else, though less than his fellow writers. For the first two or three years, the activities of the Writers' Association were suspended, with most of the professional writers being cast as "evil monsters" for having advocated the feudalist, the capitalist, and the revisionist in their writings. Thanks to Bao's working-class background, though, he was able to successfully declare that he had remained a red-hearted worker, in spite of his exposure to bourgeois influence. He joined a Red Guard organization and denounced the capitalist road cadres as well as the counterrevolutionary writers, including Xin, the head of the Writers' Association, who had brought Bao into the institution.

Bao continued to produce new poems, one of which was made into a popular song in the seventies:

> *The fish cannot swim without water.*
> *The flower cannot blossom without sunlight.*
> *And to make revolution,*
> *We cannot go without Mao Zedong Thought.*

However, Bao wrote less than before, partly because of his busy revolutionary activities, and partly because of the unpredictable political weather. In those days, anybody could become a counterrevolutionary over something as small as a couple of lines. In the early seventies, he tried to compose a poem about Mao standing together with his close comrade-in-arms and successor Lin on Tiananmen Gate, but Lin was suddenly killed—according to a red-headlined Party document—after a diabolic attempt to assassinate Mao. It was a sheer stroke of luck that the poem did not get into print: the editor had fallen sick, and Bao was able to retrieve the poem at the last minute. In the mid-seventies, however, Bao had an opportunity to concentrate on his writing without having to worry about the changing political tides. Comrade Zhang Chunqiao, then a most powerful politburo member, published an important article which criticized, among other things, bourgeoisie intellectuals by denouncing a popular saying that compared intellectuals to stinking tofu—i.e., stinking in smell, but superb in taste. The article, approved by Chair-

man Mao, became an important Party document of the
Cultural Revolution that people all over the country studied. The stinking tofu metaphor in Zhang's article was in-
spired, as it was said, by something Bao had written years
earlier, though Bao himself could hardly recall it. Bao was
selected by the Shanghai City Revolutionary Committee,
along with several others, to produce a long poem eulo-
gizing the Cultural Revolution. Bao and his fellow poets
were put in a villa on Huaihai Road—all expenses paid—
while he worked on the political assignment. This time,
things couldn't go wrong, Bao believed, and, despite its
poor sales in bookstores, he was very proud of the result, a
revolutionary epic of more than two thousand lines.

After the Cultural Revolution, things began to change
again. Xin, rehabilitated as the head of the Writers' Association, couldn't find it in his heart to forgive Bao. It was easy
to denounce Bao for his close ties to the Gang of Four, and
the revolutionary epic poem was pointed to as the undeni-
able evidence. Bao had to turn in self-criticisms even longer
than the poem. He turned out to be "tofu-spined," plead-
ing guilty to the accusations in tears. Once again, he was
spared because of his working-class status. The Party authorities didn't want to make him a target when so many
workers had begun to complain about the loss of their political glory.

When he was allowed to write again, however, a group
of young poets called Misties appeared on the scene. They
wrote in a different fashion, with obscure images that Bao

denounced as "too difficult for the working-class people to understand." Contrary to his prediction, however, the Misties turned out to be increasingly popular. Bao himself managed to hammer out one or two new poems condemning the Cultural Revolution, but no magazine would look at them.

So instead of resuming his status as a professional writer, Bao started to work as a research fellow in the Shanghai Institute of Literature Studies. In the early eighties, Mao's emphasis on the reliance of the proletarian writers still had some resonance. It was an easy job for Bao, who went to the institute only twice a week. According to his wife, it was an academic position equal to that of a university professor. He was collecting poems by workers, she explained, in the libraries and factories, though people saw him sitting by the window, hardly working.

Bao started to look less and less like a renowned poet. He frequently joined in the evening talk of the lane, sitting on an old rattan chair, waving a cattail-leaf fan, and picking his teeth with a match. He never talked about his poetry project, nor decked his speech with those literary terms.

Nor did his wife follow him around like a shadow, with a notebook and pen in hand. There was no point collecting his remarks, she declared: "They are nothing but repeated clichés." In addition to her day job teaching at a high school, in the evening she was a much-demanded private tutor for kids studying to pass the college entrance examination. In the fast-changing society, a good college education meant a lot for the future of young people, and their parents spared no expense. As a result, the combined income from her state and private employment was five or six times more than Bao's. In the market economy, it had become a matter of course for people's value to increase or decrease in relation to their income. The room once used as Bao's study became a private classroom for Mrs. Bao.

Bao's job at the institute turned out to be no "iron rice bowl" either. A new regulation was instituted, and to keep his position as a research fellow, he had to meet an annual quota of publishing more than ten thousand characters of literary criticism. No publisher, however, would consider his proposal for *Shanghai Workers' Poems*. Like other companies, publishing houses now had to look to their own balance sheets.

Perhaps that was why his wife had to teach so many students, his neighbors said. One morning, they awoke to see Bao preparing a duck in the lane sink, plucking the duck hair with a pair of steel tweezers. "She works so hard," Bao explained with a smile. "I'm going to make an old duck soup for her." He appeared to be quite handy, adding white tofu and green onion to the soup, the pleasant flavor of which soon came floating out of the common kitchen area of the *shikumen* house. That night, he served her the soup as well as a platter of duck in oyster sauce that was said to be better than the special at Xinya Restaurant. For all their years together, he simply hadn't had any opportunity to demonstrate the considerate husband in him.

Still, things between the couple began to deteriorate. Shortly after the duck dinner, she was heard to say that she was going to dump him once he was dumped by the institute of literature. She told him, "You should have stayed in Ningbo, making your tofu."

"He could have committed suicide by ramming his head against tofu," Four-Eyed Liu observed sarcastically in the evening talk.

"A couple is like two birds. When disaster comes, they have to fly in different directions," Old Root said, quoting a line from the *Dream of the Red Chamber*. "By becoming a poet, he got his position, his room, and his wife, but because of it, he's losing everything he has got . . ."

What if Bao had remained at the tofu shop in the Ningbo countryside? That was the question hovering over the lane.

So when Bao actually started his tofu business at the front of the lane, it didn't come as much of a surprise. No one bothered to ask him about his job at the institute of literature; suffice it to say that he no longer worked there. There was no point in rubbing the humiliation in. Besides, people like someone who can face adversity by grinning and bearing it.

Guo, a young student in the audience, listened to the story with great interest and launched into a harangue about a so-called dried-tofu-shaped poem: a sort of short poem with each and every line containing the same number of Chinese characters, so it looked like a piece of dried tofu. He improvised a doggerel there and then, starting, "What kind of man make what kind of tofu—"

"No, don't make fun," Old Root said, stopping Guo before he finished. "It has really come full circle, the end coming back to meet the beginning. Bao might well change the sign for his booth to read: Tofu Poet Bao's."

Foot Masseur

(1998)

This is the last issue of *Red Dust Lane Blackboard Newsletter* for the year 1998. In March, Comrade Zhu Rongji succeeded Comrade Li Peng as premier and actively sought for China's membership in the World Trade Organization. In June, American President Clinton visited China. China suffered flooding along the Yangtze and other rivers in the summer, but under the great leadership of our Party government, the Chinese people achieved victory fighting against the natural disaster. Later this year, a financial crisis broke out in Asia, and China won world respect for its economic role in the midst of it.

Black-Haired Ding's luck changed dramatically that year, as if on a roller coaster in the newly built Jingjiang Theme Park. Like everything else in the world, the turn of fortune was the result of a long chain of cause and effect. As

a Buddhist maxim says, something as small as a peck or a
sip must have been predetermined, and is then determin-
ing too.

The beginnings were all the way back in the late seventies, when White-Haired Ding, an old bachelor of Red
Dust Lane, retired from the Yangtze Bathhouse and gave
his job, as well as the *tingzijian* room, to his nephew, Black-
Haired Ding, who was then still a young boy farming in
the countryside of Jiangbei, north of the Yangtze River.
It was a special arrangement made in consideration of
the old man's status as a national model worker, one who
had been received by Chairman Mao in the sixties. Before
going back to the countryside, the old man told his nephew
only one thing.

"You can do a good job in any profession."

A bathhouse job was not considered desirable, not even
in socialist China. In the pre-1949 era, bathhouse workers
had been mostly from Jiangbei, an impoverished, backward
area that had a derogatory connotation to the Shanghainese. Black-Haired Ding's job was that of a foot masseur
by the large pool. In Mao's day, with his political doctrine
of serving the people regardless of profession, it had been
through that job that White-Haired Ding had been pro-
moted to the status of a national model worker.

The young man still considered himself lucky to be
working at a state-run bathhouse in Shanghai, with all
sorts of job benefits, instead of farming in the countryside.
Among other things, he didn't have to worry about hot

water and could bathe to his heart's content all year round, a luxury even the well-off lane residents couldn't afford. He didn't have to worry about cooking or eating at home, either. There was a large stove in the bathhouse, where employees warmed or steamed their rice, from breakfast to dinner. Last but not least, he didn't have to worry much about clothing. The moment he stepped into the bathhouse, he stripped himself naked, took a shower, and wrapped himself in a towel, which was his working uniform. It was a matter of necessity, since he spent the day massaging and sweating by the hot pool. The result was that he hardly had to buy any new clothes, and the Mao suit he had inherited from his uncle still appeared quite new after several years.

He had inherited his skill as a foot masseur from his uncle as well. It didn't take long for him to win a name for himself in the circle. Like his uncle, he seemed to develop a real passion for the job. In time, he settled into the lane, though he was still regarded as a "Jiangbeinese," because of his strong dialect.

Eventually, like others in the lane, it was time for him to think about finding a girlfriend. Through the help of Auntie Jia, he met with Linlin, a young girl working in a collective-run soy sauce shop. On the matchmaking scale of Auntie Jia, a collective-run company employee with less pay would prove to be equal to him, employee of a state-run bathhouse. Soon, Linlin was seen visiting him in the lane. Since he had a room to himself, his neighbors began holding their breath on those occasions, pricking up their ears to listen for any suspicious sound from behind the closed door of his room. The neighborhood committee also kept itself on high alert. But suddenly, Linlin didn't come anymore.

Black-Haired Ding wouldn't talk about her abrupt evaporation. Some said it was because of a mistake he made. As the story went, one afternoon she brought some fruit to his bathhouse, where, too excited by her visit, he ran out wearing nothing but a towel. She was more than embarrassed. A different version, to the surprise of the lane, also began to circulate, a story to the effect that he had a sexual orientation problem, through his long expo-sure to naked male bodies at the bathhouse. The fact that White-Haired Ding, too, had remained a bachelor all his life added credibility to the story.

Black-Haired Ding didn't seem to care too much about losing his girlfriend. Nor did he try to refute the inter-pretations of his continuing celibacy. He went to the bath-house as before, working hard, wearing the same Mao jacket.

Time flows away like the dirty water in the bathhouse.

In the years of the Cultural Revolution, there were many things far more important than speculations about Ding's possible personal problem. People in the lane didn't talk about it anymore, though it did seem to be confirmed that it was a problem.

The Cultural Revolution started with a bang and ended

with a whimper. After the passing of our great leader Chairman Mao and the stepping down of our wise leader Chairman Hua, it was our veteran leader Chairman Deng Xiaoping that started the economic reform in China. By then Black-Haired Ding had reached his thirties, having lost most of his Jiangbei accent, half of his black hair, and, as a result, his nickname too. It might have been just as well. He had long been the one and only Ding in the neighborhood. According to his occasional comments during the evening talk of the lane, he had his worries like everyone else, but all of them seemed to wash away in the hot-water pool of the bathhouse.

"After all, what's the difference between people when everyone is naked? What's the difference in the dirty bath-water?"

But in the course of the economic reform, a difference did begin to show up at the state-run bathhouse. The service at the bathhouse was now considered too low-end to be desirable by the newly rich, who preferred the "special service" performed by the young female masseuses at the privately run bathhouses. On the other hand, the state-run bathhouse was now too expensive for the newly poor, and its business went downhill. Ding was laid off with one-third pay as part of a "waiting-for-retirement program." According to the new policy, people in the program could still look for other jobs, but unlike others, Ding's skill was totally useless outside of the bathhouse.

He thought about going back to Jiangbei village, where

he might be able to eke out a living on his waiting-for-retirement pay. But after he learned that his childhood friends there were all now married with children, he changed his mind. He even began to wonder whether his uncle had really done him a favor by bringing him to the city.

But there is no predicting when someone's luck will change in this world. One of his former clients, a man who was now a Big Buck owning several companies, had infuriated his wife by enjoying himself too much in those new bathhouses. He swore to her that he was only getting foot massages, and he suggested she get her own foot massages from Ding. The Big Buck, who must have heard the rumors about Ding's sexual orientation, made him a lucrative offer.

"Prove to my wife the miraculous effects of foot massage. You may come to our house to do this."

So Ding went. It was a grand new mansion, and the Big Buck's wife was like a goddess wrapped in a white robe, coming from the bathroom, her footprints lotus-flower-like on the hardwood floor. Why the Big Buck would fool around with such a wife at home, Ding couldn't imagine. But what occupied him right then was something else, something more immediate and intimate. Her bare feet were so perfect it was as if they were carved out of soft white jade, and her toenails so like petals trembling in his lap that he could barely hold the manicuring knife steady. Some people would have paid a bundle of money just to touch her little toe, so glistening, soft, and white, like peeled fresh lychee. Still, he managed to do a good job with the massage, and she tipped him handsomely.

And she requested that he come back and provide foot massages again, and again. Afterward, he could occasionally enjoy a free shower while she fell asleep on the sofa, her feet thoroughly massaged and looking like white jade on red velvet. It was almost like the good old days when he first came to Shanghai, except for one difference—the shower he took was a quick, cold one, which he used to dampen his excitement.

Soon his name spread among a widening group of rich ladies. With the rumors about his sexual orientation taken for granted, they welcomed him into their homes—like a eunuch into the royal palace. One insisted on enjoying Ding's massage while in the bedroom, stretching her feet out against the dower pillow while talking on the phone; another actually summoned him into the bathroom, luxuriating in the bathtub while placing her toes like rose petals into his hands. From time to time, the sultry, sweating scenes became too much for him. But he knew he had to control himself.

He also had to dress properly now. He wore some special baggy pants, which seemed exotic to the people in the lane, but he couldn't tell anyone the real reason for it. He was worried that his secret would be discovered by those ladies, and he couldn't afford any mistakes.

But other than that, he considered himself the luckiest SOB under the sun. He made good money, bringing home in a couple of evenings more than his former monthly salary at the state-run bathhouse. It was an easy and fantastic job, his eyes feasting on the sight of those naked or half-naked women, their dainty toes wriggling in his grasp, their shapely soles like soft dough to be kneaded to his heart's content.

The neighbors in the lane began to notice some conspicuous changes about him and began to ask questions.

"Have you made a fortune, Ding?"

"Do you have a girlfriend, Ding?"

The first question was rhetorical, and the second, not as much. But if he'd had a girlfriend, he would have brought her to the lane. So, eventually, people went back to the old assumptions about his sexual orientation.

According to a new Chinese saying, money burns a man. With all the money that he now had in his pocket, Ding was burning with desire, and the constant parade of naked beauties didn't help.

He thought about finding a girlfriend, but with his dubious reputation, no one wanted to introduce any girls to him. Nor could he try the new "personals" column in the *Wenhui Daily*. If news of that were to get out, he could lose all his customers.

Then he remembered the stories about the foot massage service in those private bathhouses. He was curious about it, wondering how those young girls could do their jobs without any training. Anyway, he could well afford it, he thought, as long as he didn't go too far.

So one afternoon he went to a new bathhouse. According to the service menu on the wall, foot massage alone was not that expensive.

A tall man with a big beard approached him at the entrance. "A girl?"

Ding simply nodded.

"Double expense?"

He did not really understand what that meant, but he nodded again, deciding not to say too much lest he reveal how inexperienced he was.

A young skinny girl led him to a cubicle, where he was told to lie down on a narrow bed. She removed his shoes, pulled his feet into a basin of hot water, and massaged his feet. She didn't have much skill, but her soft fingers made the difference, especially when she started scratching and scraping the callous on his heel with her bare nails. In his professional experience, that was something to be done with a special file. He was touched, and his mind was still wandering when she said, "Pull down your pants?"

He barely nodded, not knowing what to say or do. Without taking off her own clothes, she pulled down his pants, leaned over, and started licking and sucking before taking him into her mouth.

She must have gargled with a magic liquid, for her mouth became warm, almost hot as she increased her tempo. It was more than he could humanly endure. He was exploding into her mouth, when several cops burst into the cubicle, catching him in the act of engaging in this illegal service.

What happened in the next few hours was like a night-mare, one in which he was totally paralyzed, unable to speak or act. He was aware of being held in custody for the night at a nearby police station, but it was as if it were hap-pening to another man, like a fast rewinding of a broken videotape in the dark.

The next morning he was released, because of his lack of any previous criminal history, but the police dutifully passed the information on to the neighborhood commit-tee of Red Dust Lane. It was then up to the committee to decide on the proper punishment, which could come in the form of a neighborhood criticism meeting, where Ding would have to make a confession with all the vivid details. But Comrade Jun, the head of the committee, hesi-tated and hurried over to discuss it with Old Root.

"What rotten luck. To be caught the first time!" the old man said. "Still, it may be a timely lesson for him."

"But what are we going to do?"

"If the story comes out, it will mean a big loss of face for him, but there might be some positive effect. At least, he will prove himself to be a man, and in the neighbor-hood, all the stories about him might disappear overnight. But what if word got out of the neighborhood?"

"That's the question." Comrade Jun said, nodding. "That's why I wanted to consult you."

"His service depends on people's belief in the rumors. Once the word got around, his career would be over."

"Exactly. And there are already so many unemployed

in the neighborhood, that it's becoming an increasing lia-bility to the committee. But there has to be some punish-ment. I have to report back to the district police station."

"Wasn't there a campaign against bourgeois liberalism a couple of years ago? What about punishing him in the name of it?" Old Root said. "Make it about all his fancy new clothes—the baggy pants with so many pockets. I've heard that it's part of a new American style, hip-hop."

"Great idea, Old Root. You're a genius. 'Bourgeois liber-alism' is really a perfect umbrella word. Never outdated, and proper and right for Ding."

Father and Son

(2000)

This is the last issue of *Red Dust Lane Blackboard Newsletter* for the year 2000. China successfully launched the Chinasat-22 communication satellites. With the introduction of the Internet into our daily life, the government has consolidated the Internet regulations. President Jiang Zemin delivered his important talk about the "Three Represents" as the guideline for Party work. Our Party authorities intensified the crackdown on official corruption with the execution of a former deputy chairman of the National People's Congress for bribe-taking. This year also witnessed the beginning of the population resettlement required for the Three Gorges Dam project. China's GDP grew by eight percent for the year.

"Look at the picture. He's still so young, with his Young Pioneer's Red Scarf shining in the golden sunlight of

socialist China," Comrade Kang said with difficulty, coughing with a fist pressed against his mouth. He sat as stiff as
a bamboo stick at the entrance of Red Dust Lane, turning
over a page in the old photo album.

Why Comrade Kang insisted on coming out and showing us the picture that evening in spite of his poor health
was something we thought we knew. It was because his
son, Big Buck Kang, had turned out the opposite of what his
father expected of him—he didn't become "a worthy successor to the great cause of communism." Comrade Kang
was devastated, not just by his son, but by the way things
were developing in the country too. He simply wanted to
go over these years one more time, in another attempt to
justify his own lifelong pursuit. Given his deteriorating
health, he probably would not have too many more evenings like that with us. So we sat around him, waving our
cattail-leaf fans to the rhythm of the evening talk.

Comrade Kang joined the Communist Party in 1948, one
year before the liberation of Shanghai. In the early fifties,
he was assigned to work as the director of a large textile
factory. He devoted himself to the work—to the transformation of the factory into a state-run one with all the benefits of socialism (job security and medical benefits for the
employees) and to increasing production in accordance to
the state plan. As a midlevel Party cadre, in the early sixties, he could have moved out of Red Dust Lane to a larger

apartment, but he insisted on modeling himself after the selfless Comrade Lei Feng and gave the opportunity to somebody else. With the outbreak of the Cultural Revolution, however, overnight he was turned into a "capitalist roader" and made to wear around his neck a huge blackboard with his name crossed out. He was then sent to a "cadre school," to reform him through hard labor. His wife died the second year, leaving their only son alone in the city. Comrade Kang didn't return home until almost the end of the Cultural Revolution, a shrunken shadow of the former Bolshevik, dragging a crippled leg, and a total stranger to his son, who had grown up on his own.

"In the long history of humankind, socialism as a new system could not avoid experiencing some bumps along the way," Comrade Kang said sincerely to his son, quoting verbatim from the *People's Daily*. "We should never lose faith in our Party, in our system."

He had barely been rehabilitated as the factory director, however, when, in the mid-eighties, the new cadre retirement policy came into practice. He stepped down, making no attempt to hang on to his position. He also made a point of not going back to the factory frequently. He knew better than to interfere with the new director's work, though he couldn't help worrying about the new problems there.

In short, he had lived up to his ideal of a loyal Party member all those years. In his opinion, there was only one exception: he agreed to accept monetary compensation for his loss during the Cultural Revolution. He took the money to purchase a plane ticket for his son, who, in the mid-eighties, wanted to go to a language school in Japan. Comrade Kang didn't like the idea, but his son said he had lost the opportunity to go to school here—because Comrade Kang had been labeled a "capitalist roader" in the seventies.

The father had felt guilty about what had happened to the son. What really upset Comrade Kang, however, was the change in his son after the young man's return from Japan.

The son turned out to be totally different from his father. In Japan, instead of taking the required classes, he worked at any kind of odd job he could find, saving his money like an old miser. While many people were leaving China in the late eighties, he came back to China with a small amount of capital, declaring that he saw great opportunities there for his business.

"In Japan, their business regulations are firmly established, with no large loopholes that allow one to maneuver. But things are quite different here, with opportunities for men with money to invest," he said. "The Chinese government is now encouraging private business as a supplement to the state economy. Everything is new." So he started his business, a huge seafood restaurant in the Qibao suburb. In those years, there weren't many restaurants in the city, and the state-run restaurants hadn't changed their menus for over twenty years. He introduced a new service.

In his restaurant, live seafood was displayed in glass cages like in a market—fishes, shrimps, lobsters, crabs—and the customers could choose for themselves. Their choices would be weighed, prepared, and cooked in accordance to their specific requests. This gave the customers the impression that they were getting seafood of better quality and, overall, a better bargain. Practical Shanghainese started to swarm his restaurant, and soon they had to take a number and wait in line to be seated.

"Come to my restaurant. Fifty percent discount," Big Buck Kang offered expansively one night during the evening talk in front of the lane.

"But then how could you make money?"

"I don't need to make money off of you, my old neighbors. Now it's the age of 'socialist business expense.' It is fashionable and politically correct for Party cadres to spend their company's money dining and entertaining in the name of socialist business expense—and all for their personal benefit. Since it is not their own money, they can afford to throw it away like water. They are the customers that are my gold mines. I have quite a few private rooms set aside for socialist business expense customers." He added, "Good, honest people like my father are becoming fewer and fewer. He has dedicated his life to the Party, but for what? Well, don't say anything to the old man—about socialist business expense or anything else."

We didn't. We later learned that, for his socialist business expense customers, Big Buck Kang had special receipts in addition to special rooms. For an eight hundred yuan meal, they could get a receipt adding up to three thousand. So his restaurant customers continued to snowball. How much he was really making, we had no clue. Soon he moved to a fancy apartment in the Upper Corner of the city. He tried to talk his father into moving with him, but the old man said no.

When other private restaurants with similar practices began opening, Big Buck Kang, to the surprise of the lane, shifted to the karaoke business.

"Karaoke is a very popular entertainment in Japan," he explained. "You sing along to the music with captions for the words running on the TV screen."

"Come on, Big Buck Kang. Do you really think Shanghainese will pay to sing a song?" one of his former neighbors asked. "We can sing to our hearts' content at home or in the evening at the front of the lane, without having to pay a penny."

"For one thing, whether Japanese or Chinese, Asian people don't let go of their inhibitions so easily. Karaoke provides a sort of social convention, allowing them to do whatever they are normally too inhibited to do." Big Buck Kang added with a mysterious smile, "Besides, a karaoke club may meet the needs of people in a number of ways."

People didn't believe in his theory, but he believed in himself. He lost no time converting an old building into a karaoke hall with a number of private rooms. It proved to be another huge hit. Evidently, Chinese people were no longer satisfied simply with a meal, no matter how expensive or fabulous. As a Confucian sage said two thousand years ago, "When you are well fed and clad, your mind goes astray." Karaoke became a trend, a "must" in the city, especially for those who had "become rich first," as Comrade Deng Xiaoping phrased it.

Customers went there not just for karaoke, but for something else under the cover of karaoke. Hotels still required a marriage certificate for a couple to check in together, so the private karaoke rooms with their locked doors met the understood yet unstated needs of the city. Soon, "karaoke girls" appeared, supposedly to sing for the customers. When the door was locked, however, whatever other services they might provide could be easily imagined.

Inevitably, stories about those karaoke girls reached the lane—and Comrade Kang flew into a rage.

"Don't worry about it, Father," the son said. "Our business is law-abiding. The Jin'an Police Station is located only five minutes away. If we allowed anything improper, they would come rushing over."

But that was only partially true. The police chief of Jin'an district was a regular of the karaoke club. To be fair to Big Buck Kang, he was a filial son, trying hard to appease the old man. He said to us in the lane, "What's the point in arguing with your father? It's like arguing with history."

Another reason for him not to argue with his father was that the old man's health was declining. The reform of the state medical insurance didn't help. In the past, retirees of state-run companies had enjoyed full medical coverage; now the coverage had been drastically cut. His annual coverage now was capped at eight hundred yuan, which barely covered his heart medicine for three months. Instead of accepting the money offered by his son, he tried to cut down his medical expense.

Because of his extraordinary karaoke business, Big Buck Kang couldn't come back to the lane as often as he would have liked. So he asked us for our help in taking care of the old man. To show his appreciation, he invited some of us to his club, where we were treated like princes, with the karaoke girls singing and dancing to our hearts' content. At the hourly price of three hundred yuan for an evening in a high-class private room, plus all the food and drink, the bill would normally have been staggering. People in the lane calculated that bill and talked about that evening for days. Since most of the clients there were upstart entrepreneurs or government cadres, they could be liberal in their spending, and the club's nightly revenue could be as high as six figures. That was even without including all the other gray money—such as the percentage those karaoke girls kicked back from their "private service fee."

As China's economic reform progressed, Big Buck Kang made another business decision that confounded all of us in the lane, except for Comrade Kang, who was now in the hospital. The decision was about the very textile factory for which the old man had worked for more than thirty years.

The factory had been in terrible shape for a long time. In the old state-economy system, the factory simply manufactured whatever was required in accordance to the government orders, regardless of any profit or loss. Now the factory had to compete for survival in the open market and was fully responsible for the workers' pay and benefits. Director Fei, the director after Comrade Kang, turned out to be clueless as to handling the problems now besieging the factory. Their products were substandard and were no longer marketable, let alone profitable. The workers, having been "iron rice bowl holders" for so many years, could do little to help. The large number of pensioners on their books became an increasingly unbearable burden. Fei was becoming as desperate as an ant crawling on a hot wok.

But Fei wasn't alone in facing these problems. Throughout the country, more than half of the state-run factories were in deep trouble, some nearing bankruptcy. According to the *People's Daily*, this was "inevitable in the historic transition from the state economy to the market economy." Whatever the official interpretations, the government had given up subsidizing those factories. A new policy was generated instead: a state-run company could apply for bankruptcy and its employees could be sent home with a onetime compensation. Interested entrepreneurs were encouraged to buy such companies and were offered a huge discount if they retained some of the employees for at least two years.

That special clause reduced the government compensation for factories, it was argued, but contributed to political stability by reducing unemployment numbers.

When Comrade Kang's factory was put on the list of factories for sale, the buyer turned out to be none other than Big Buck Kang. After he agreed to keep about two hundred employees, he got the factory for only a "symbolic sum." In the logic of the new age, this kind of transaction was a good thing. The state would stop losing money, and some of the now–state employees would hold onto their rice bowl—at least for a couple of years more.

There was one concession that Big Buck Kang refused to make in the negotiations. It was about the pensions and benefits of the retired employees, none of which he would take on. The only exception was the former executives. As for Comrade Kang, Big Buck Kang included him in the executive severance package, which meant that, as an ex-executive, the old man would still enjoy his pension and benefits as before.

What astonished us was his secret business plan, which was revealed after the conclusion of the deal. He mortgaged the factory for five or six times more than what he'd paid for it. Then he unveiled plans to raze the factory to make way for housing construction. It turned out to be close to a planned subway route, so his proposal attracted a large number of investors. Also, he reached an agreement of joint development with a real estate contractor, through which he was able to keep his part of the original deal with the government by retaining those two hundred employees as temporary construction workers. At the end of construction, he would own one third of the whole apartment complex.

It was one arrow that killed several birds. It helped the state by getting rid of a financial burden, kept two hundred workers' pots boiling—at least for the next couple of years—and would help meet the housing needs of the city.

Not to mention the unbelievable profits it would generate for Big Buck Kang.

Questions arose in the lane like bees swarming out of an upset hive.

"It's like catching a white fox with one's bare hands," Old Hunchback Fang commented in indignation. "He hasn't paid a single penny out of his pocket."

"Why was it impossible for Fei to have done that?" Four-Eyed Liu joined in. "At least then the workers could have shared some of the profits. And later perhaps some of the housing too."

But Big Buck Kang wasn't willing to discuss the deal with us, saying that he had to see his father, who had just come home from the hospital. He was a good son and was trying to keep the old man in the dark.

But Comrade Kang wasn't going to have a peaceful evening, examining the pictures of his son in childhood. A retired worker from his factory came stumbling into the lane. She wanted to air her grievances to the "Comrade Director Kang" without knowing anything about his illness. Emotionally distraught, she started sobbing and complaining to him in front of the whole lane.

"Oh Comrade Director Kang, you should have never retired. Do you know what Fei has done to our factory? That bastard has squandered away state property for his personal benefit. His severance package for selling the factory came to six figures."

"Selling the factory!" Comrade Kang was stunned.

"What's more, he got a fat red envelope under the table—a certificate for a three-bedroom apartment when the construction project on the site of our good old factory is done. It's really a changed world, Comrade Kang. It's just like going back to the old society over one night. The black-hearted, big-buck capitalist, who bought our good old factory for nothing, is wallowing in money, and we workers are suffering—it's like we're in an abyss of scorching fire and freezing water. Alas, Chairman Mao's dead, and you're retired, who is going to take care of poor retired workers like us?"

Comrade Kang, having been in and out of the hospital of late, was totally oblivious of what had happened to the factory. Listening to her, he broke out in a cold sweat, slipped from the bamboo chair, and passed out on the curb in front of the lane.

That evening, after we rushed Comrade Kang back to the hospital, we prayed for his recovery. But then we worried about his reaction when he woke up and learned all the details about the destruction of "the good old factory," particularly the role Big Buck Kang had played in it.

Little Hao, a young member of the evening talk of Red Dust Lane, was less pessimistic. "What's the big deal? If the factory was once the father's, it's now the son's—at least, all the value of it."

Confucius and Crab

(2001)

This is the last issue of *Red Dust Lane Blackboard Newsletter* for the year 2001. It was another year of great achievements for the Chinese people. In spite of a diplomatic standoff over the detention of an American spy plane and crew after a midair collision with a Chinese fighter jet earlier in the year, China made huge progress in its international relations. In June, leaders of China, Russia, and four Central Asian states launched the Shanghai Cooperation Organization and signed an agreement to promote trade and investment. In July, Beijing was awarded the 2008 Olympic Games, which spoke eloquently for the enhanced status of China in today's world. In November, after years of negotiation, China joined the World Trade Organization.

It was crab season again. Aiguo, a retired middle school teacher who lived in Red Dust Lane, couldn't help casting another glance toward the neighborhood seafood market in the afternoon sunlight. There was no point stopping in for a look at the live crabs crawling in cages, since he couldn't afford to buy even one in the new millennium. Indeed, Confucius says: *time flows away like water.* Memories rise to the top like algae in a pond.

Five or six years before the economic reform started in the eighties, Aiguo was so disappointed with the banishment of Confucius from the classroom that he began to develop a crab complex. He made a point of enjoying the Yangchen river crabs three or four times during each crab season. His wife had passed away, and his son had just started working in a state-run steel plant and was dating a young girl, so Aiguo justified his one and only passion by referencing well-known writers like Su Dongpo, a Song dynasty poet, who declared a crab feast the most blissful moment of his life—"O that I could have crabs without a wine supervisor sitting beside me"—or like Li Yu, a Ming dynasty scholar, who confessed that he wrote for the purpose of earning "crab money"—his "life-saving money." As an intellectual immersed in what "Confucius says," Aiguo had to restrain himself from lecturing about the sage in public in those days, but he used the sage's ritualistic rules for crab-eating at home.

"Do not eat when the food is rotten; do not eat when it looks off-color; do not eat when it smells bad; do not eat when it is not properly cooked; do not eat when it is off season; do no eat when it is not cut right; do not eat when it is not served with the appropriate sauce . . . Do not throw away the ginger . . . Be serious and solemn when one offers a sacrifice meal to his ancestors . . .' " Aiguo would quote from the *Analects* by Confucius over a platter of steaming hot crab, adding, "It's about the live Yangcheng crabs, really, about all the necessary requirements for them, including a piece of ginger."

"All are but excuses for his crab craziness. Confucius says," his son commented to the neighbors with a resigned shrug. "You don't have to listen to him."

Indeed, Aiguo suffered from a characteristic crab syndrome: as soon as the western wind rose in November, it was as if his heart were being pinched and scratched by crab claws. He had to conquer the craving with "a couple of the Yangcheng River crabs, a cup of yellow wine," before he was able to work hard for another year, full of energy for whatever "Confucius says," until the next crab season.

Aiguo retired just as the economic reform was picking up steam in the nineties, when the price of crab started to rocket. A pound of large crabs would cost three hundred yuan, which was more than half of his monthly pension. Crabs became a luxury affordable only by the newly rich in this society in transition. For the majority of the Shanghai crab eaters like Aiguo, crab season became almost a torture.

In the same *shikumen* house lived Gengbao, a former

student of Aiguo's. Gengbao hardly acknowledged Aiguo as his teacher, since he had flunked out of school, having gotten a number of D's and F's from Aiguo. As it is said in *Tao Te Ching*, "In misfortune comes fortune." Because he failed at school, Gengbao started a cricket business and made a small fortune. In Shanghai, people gambled on cricket fights, so a ferocious cricket could sell for thousands of yuan. Gengbao was able to catch the fiercest crickets from a "secret cemetery," a place from where the crickets, having absorbed the infernal spirits, fought like devils. It proved to be a lucrative niche market. Even after making a fortune, he chose not to move away from his attic room in Red Dust Lane, since he believed its feng shui had brought his fortune. So he stayed on, living next door to Aiguo, despite having bought a new apartment somewhere else in the city. In the old building, he shared the common kitchen, as well as a common passion, with Aiguo: the crab. Gengbao enjoyed crabs to his heart's content and made a big show of it, parading crabs through the kitchen, nailing crab shells like monster masks on the wall above the coal briquette stove. Aiguo suffered through all of this, sighing and quoting from a Confucian classic, "It's the teacher's fault to have not taught a student properly."

"What do you mean?" Aiguo's daughter-in-law responded. "Gengbao is a Big Buck nowadays. Your ancestors must have burned tall incense for you to have taught such a successful student."

If there was any cold comfort for Aiguo of late, it was

that he was able to talk about Confucius openly again. But, being retired, he could only give his lecture to his grandson, Xiaoguo, an elementary school student. The array of the mysterious crab shells on the kitchen wall seemed to appeal more to Xiaoguo, who had never tasted a crab before.

"You have taught me so many things about Confucius. But what does a crab taste like, Grandpa?"

That was an impossible question for the retired teacher to answer. There is no way to taste a crab without putting it into the mouth. Aiguo adored his grandson, and as Confucius says, "You have to try to do what you should do, even though it's impossible to do so." Finally, he managed to demonstrate—to an extent—how delicious a crab could possibly be by concocting the special crab sauce of black vinegar, sugar, ginger slice, and soy sauce.

"It's somewhat like that," Aiguo said, letting Xiaoguo dip a chopstick into the sauce and suck the tip of the chopstick, "but much better, Xiaoguo."

Unexpectedly, from there Aiguo began to obsess over finding a way to satisfy his crab craving; all the crab-rich memories had come back to him the moment the sauce on the chopstick tip touched his tongue. He experimented further by stir-frying the egg yolk and white separately in a wok and then mixing them with the special sauce. The result was something redolent of the celebrated fried crab meat at Wangbaohe Restaurant. To his greater surprise, even small shrimp or dried tofu dipped in the special sauce could occasionally produce a similar effect. On those days when he could not find anything in the refrigerator, which was under the surveillance of his daughter-in-law, he would simply dip the chopsticks in and out of the special sauce, sip at his yellow wine, and chew the ginger slices.

Needless to say, all the experiments merely added to the curiosity of the close-observing Xiaoguo, who kept asking crab-related questions of Aiguo.

"Living in a poor lane, and dipping in nothing but crab sauce, one can still enjoy life," Aiguo, seemingly lost in Confucius again, said to his bewildered grandson, "Confucius says something very close to that about one of his best students . . ."

That afternoon, suffocating from those memories, Aiguo was shuffling within sight of the *shikumen* house in Red Dust Lane when, even at a distance, he smelled something like trouble. Stepping in, he saw his grandson Xiaoguo washing his hat in the sink in the common kitchen—and to Aiguo's consternation, a red crab shell nailed on the white wall. So he started questioning Xiaoguo.

As it turned out, that morning, Xiaoguo passed by a new house with the door open and caught sight of people busily preparing a huge banquet of sacrifice to their ancestors. It must have been a rich family, as there were so many luxurious cars parked in front, and there were also scripture-chanting monks hired from a Buddhist temple. He couldn't help taking a closer look. To his surprise, he saw a crab scurrying out of the front door and to the side-walk. It must have escaped from the kitchen in the midst of all of the confusion. So like a streak of lightning, Xiaoguo took off his hat and picked up the vicious-looking crab. Instead of going to school, he ran back home and prepared the special sauce, after a fashion, and boiled the crab. After devouring it without really tasting it, he painted a multicol-ored face on the crab shell with a Chinese character be-neath it—"Swear." Then he hung the shell like a primitive mask on the wall.

"How can you skip school for a crab?" Aiguo snapped, and he slapped his grandson in fury. "And a stray crab from others' offering to their ancestors too! That's against the Confucian rites. What's more, you put the crab in your hat. Now, in accordance to the rites, one of Confucius's students had to straighten up his hat before dying."

"I don't want to die, Grandpa."

Aiguo softened as Xiaoguo wept so bitterly, almost incoherently. "Study hard, Xiaoguo. When you enter the college, I'll buy crabs for you."

"What's the point?" Xiaoguo said, sobbing and smack-ing his lips. "Both you and Father studied at college, but you can't afford crabs."

"Then what are you going to do?"

"I'll be a Big Buck, and then I'll buy crabs for you. Tons of crabs, I swear. That's why I pledged on the crab shell."

"Confucius says—"

"Crap!"

Eating and Drinking Salesman

(2003)

This is the last issue of *Red Dust Lane Blackboard News-letter* for the year 2003. Early in the year, the NPC elected Hu Jintao president, replacing Jiang Zemin, who stepped down after ten years in the post. China and Hong Kong were hit by the pneumonia-like SARS: the Party government imposed strict quarantine measures to stop the disease from spreading, and the Chinese people successfully stood the test. In June, the sluice gates on Three Gorges Dam, the world's largest hydropower project, were closed to allow the reservoir to fill up. This year, China also launched its first manned spacecraft into orbit with astronaut Yang Liwei.

Wei has never been a role model in Red Dust Lane, even less so at the beginning of the new century.

Look at his potbelly, and the answer looks back at you. It's a product of excessive eating and drinking.

According to his self-justification, he overindulges because he was born in 1960, in the middle of the so-called three years of natural disasters, which spanned 1959 to 1961. It's an open secret now that during that period, more than thirty million people died of starvation—not because of any flood or drought, as was claimed in the Party newspapers, but because the Three Red Flags movement launched by Chairman Mao wrecked the national economy. Without getting into the historic details, Wei declared that, as a result of having starved inhumanly in his mother's belly, he was born with a wolfish appetite. Indeed, he was different, capable of devouring five bowls of rice with a piece of pickled cabbage, all the while dreaming of delicacies for his supersensitive palate. In short, he is a born gourmand and gourmet on top of being a glutton.

People have long concluded that he was born in the wrong time, and to the wrong family. Both his parents were ordinary workers, and for many years it remained out of the question for him to be able to satisfy his epicurean needs. Eventually, he grew up to be an ordinary worker too.

Still, Wei managed to enjoy eating and drinking in his way, or in whatever way affordable. On a summer evening, he would pull out a bamboo chair and sit on the doorstep with the chair in front serving as a dining table. He would forget all his worries over a bowl of steaming

rice. Slices of pork ears or a couple of chicken feet made it
a wonderful evening for him, and a smoked carp head and
a bottle of beer, a blissful weekend. When out of money,
he could wolf down three bowls of white rice with a pinch
of fried rice.

As for his sealike drinking capacity, that was more of a
mystery. His parents didn't drink, absolutely not during
the year of his conception. At five or six months old, Wei
had already started licking at the Shaoxin yellow rice wine
on the tip of his uncle's chopstick. Upon graduation from
high school, he ranked number one among the drinkers
in the lane, even though he was never drunk. He established himself as such during a bet with Fatty Peng. He
finished twelve bottles of Qingdao beer in one sitting, winning the bet hands down without belching once or his face
changing color.

He also liked to join in the evening talk of the lane. It
was a good audience, even if he was not a good narrator,
and he invariably turned to his favorite subject: food and
drink. Confucius says, to eat and mate is human nature,
so one cannot be too fastidious about food—or talking
about food. What he talked about, however, was hardly
exciting enough to make a story. After all, he had little
real gourmet experience to draw upon. One evening, he
suddenly came up with some surprising details about legendary dishes, such as the Beggar's Chicken or the Imperial Concubine's Duck. Since he couldn't have possibly
been able to afford them, we realized he had picked up

the tidbits from books. He had to assuage his hunger and curiosity by reading.

Anyway, after eating and drinking for thirty years, he summed up his philosophy with a handful of roasted sunflower seeds.

"My philosophy is simple: there're things I don't do, and things I do. I don't gamble. Those mahjong players lose everything, including their own pants. I don't sleep around. Those suckers throw their money into bottomless holes, and sometimes their lives as well. If I have money, I eat and drink. Life is short. Enjoy it the most practical way you can. You dress for others to see, but you eat for yourself to be. Anyway, you do not let your stomach down. Some eat to live, I live to eat. For me, that's what life is all about."

"What a wine sack and a rice bag!" Four-Eyed Liu commented, quoting a Chinese proverb about a man good at nothing except eating and drinking.

Whatever others might have thought, Wei then met Mei, a young girl who liked him—his potbelly was half its current size at the time—and they got married.

In due time, they had a daughter named Lei, whose arrival began to bring changes into his life. To start with, people no longer saw any meat or fish on top of his rice. If occasionally he still had beer, it was the cheap watery liquid from a side-street eatery that pumped air bubbles into the barrel.

The daughter was both like, yet not like, the father.

While still a toddler, Lei developed an extraordinary passion for food, but only for non-Chinese food. Born in a different time, with Western supermarkets and fast-food restaurants popping up like mushrooms everywhere in the city, she took an inexplicable liking to McDonald's. At the age of four, she could gulp down two Big Macs with an extra large French fries for lunch, plus a tall cup of Coca-Cola. She refused to touch rice or steamed buns, the common homely stuff in Red Dust Lane. A Big Mac cost almost a day's wage for Wei, whose company kept cutting the employee's pay because of fierce market competition. To do him justice, he was a good father who never grumbled about the expense of raising Lei, which was ever-increasing as she grew into a plump teenager with engaging dimples.

But Mei couldn't help grumbling. After all those years in the factory, Wei was still a worker at the lowest level, making one third less than others who had started working about the same time. Nevertheless, Wei considered himself lucky: the director of the factory was Dapei, who, having lived in the neighborhood for quite a few years, was an elementary schoolmate of Wei's. Otherwise, Wei could have been laid off long ago.

"All you know how to do is to eat and drink," Mei complained bitterly out in the lane, "with the mountain turning barren and the river running dry. And I have the two of you on my hands—like father, like daughter."

According to Karl Marx, the superstructure is dependent on the economic basis. A wife who displays the virtue of making no complaint may well be construed as part of the superstructure, so there was nothing Wei could do about it. But things went from bad to worse. A considerable number of state-run companies slipped to the brink of bankruptcy. People had to find new jobs elsewhere. Wei, with no special skills or education on his resume, worried like an ant crawling around a hot wok on the fire.

Then, to the surprise of the lane, Wei managed to obtain a new position at the factory—as a salesman. All of a sudden, we began to see him leave the house in a three-piece suit tailored for his job, his moussed hair shining, and then come back home in a taxi at the end of the day, his face red like General Guan in the *Romance of the Three Kingdoms*.

Wei had never worked as a salesman before, and everyone was curious about his qualifications. He might be talkative amidst his neighbors, but he was far from persuasive in public. One evening, we caught Wei stepping out of a taxi smelling of liquor, and we asked him.

"Well, it is a story you wouldn't have imagined," Wei started, loosening his floral silk tie as he finished a chunk of dark chocolate. "In the economic reform, our state-run factory has been losing ground to those private-run ones. Those entrepreneurs are capable of anything. So Dapei decided that we had to double our PR effort to increase sales."

"What's so special about PR?" Four-Eyed Liu said, imitating a character in a movie. " 'Have a cigarette, I insist. I'll have one of yours later. Raise your glass and forget about the rules. Once the chopsticks start dipping into the dishes, everything's discussable—on the table and under it, too.' "

"That movie must have been made some time ago," Wei said with a broad grin. "Or the director doesn't know anything about doing business today. Now, the 'feast of socialist business expense' might have appealed to some customers several years ago, but soon they began to complain about it—too much to eat and drink."

"What else?" Four-Eyed Liu went on doggedly. "PR girls, karaoke girls, three-accompaniment girls—whatever names you want to call them? So you must be arranging for these girls, 'Come to the private room, treat my customer from head to foot, collect your money afterwards.' "

"That's something you don't understand. PR girls aren't like tiger-bone plasters, one size fits all. Some of our customers are sophisticated Big Bugs and Big Bucks, self-conscious about their public images. If they want girls, they can easily arrange for them without having a third party in the middle."

"What the hell do you do then, Wei?"

"I eat and drink with them."

"That's what I have just said—nothing but chicken, duck, fish, and meat in your potbelly."

"No, there are more things in heaven and earth than in your imagination in Red Dust Lane. Really, for me it started in a most unexpected way. Our factory had to invite a crucial customer to dinner. The sales manager was worried sick. Dapei thought it was necessary to have someone presentable at the table, someone knowledge-able about eating and drinking. So he thought of me. You make fun of my big belly, but for a middle-aged man like me, it's not only symbolic of success, but full of expertise too. While it is important to order an expensive dinner, that's only the first step. Far more important is to convince the customers that they are special to you, to make them eat and drink in a way they have never experienced before. Only then can the business connection be developed. For such a banquet, snakes or cats are way too common, so you have to choose an Australian wild cat or an African poi-sonous snake. Believe it or not, last week I arranged an in-sect feast that a customer loved. It was a meal of fried cicada skins and silkworm cocoons, among other things. You have to be really creative. A tiny dish of wild shepherd's purse blossom can make a world of difference in the midst of all the meat and fish. And a Tang dynasty anecdote about the chef's special will help a lot too. But first and foremost, you yourself have to eat and drink, talking and entertaining from the beginning to the end."

"It's a job made for you," Old Root commented, raising his teacup like he was proposing a toast. "As Li Bai said in one of his poems, a man is born into the world with talents to be discovered and used."

"Let me tell you something about drinking as a sales-man." Wei appeared to be in no hurry to finish, taking a sip from Old Root's teacup. "It's not as simple as raising your cup. Customers, especially those from the Northern provinces, take a hell of a lot of pride in their drinking. The more cups, the more guts. They see it as a huge loss of face if you refuse to drink. It's a time-honored tradition, you know. It's proper and right for Chinese people at the dinner table to coax or coerce each other into their cups. Dapei's face flushes like a coxswain with the first cup, and his legs wobble like a limp goose with the second. So it's up to me to sit there, drinking like an ox, playing *huaquan*—the hand game—for wine. You know *huaquan*, don't you? *Two, two good brothers. Four, fortune for four seasons.* You drain the cup if you lose. More often than not, I have to lose, bottom up, so the customers will be happy. Guess how I can drink like that? I eat a lot beforehand. So the alcohol is absorbed into the food in my stomach. When the customers chuckle in their cups, and the connection is established, the contract becomes something like a small dish."

Luck had truly fallen into Wei's lap. His specialties were finally appreciated and, more importantly, paid for too. We were all happy for him.

Mei did not appear to be too happy, though, at least not as much as we supposed she would be. "It's a hell of a job," she said, eating alone in the lane. "He comes back so late every night, and totally beaten, like a pile of dog dung."

We were puzzled. It might be common for wives to complain about their husbands coming home late. It could be an understandable concern, especially if the husband was a successful entrepreneur, with all the young pretty girls

available in "the socialist business world of China's characteristics." But Mei did not have to worry about Wei, who
was nothing but a salesman whose only value lay in eating
and drinking—he was big-bellied but empty-pocketed.
No girl could possibly fall for him. So she was asked for
an explanation.

"I would rather have him here holding a bowl of watery
rice in the lane—a simple meal with us, without all the
pressure."

But her explanation sounded not persuasive. It wasn't
easy to find a job, let alone such a mouthwatering one. She
was nagging too much.

There were many things happening in Red Dust Lane.
Wei's fantastic job, eating and drinking as a salesman,
would not have made a story but for what happened one
night several months later.

It was a September night, shortly after two A.M., and an
ambulance came wailing into the lane. Wei was then seen
being carried out of his home on a stretcher. His wife and
daughter followed them to the lane entrance, weeping.

Wei had never complained of any health problems, except for having gained more weight of late. We were worried that it could have been a heart attack.

But it wasn't. Mei hemmed and hawed without telling
us what went wrong. Two days later, Wei came back home
from the hospital. A number of his colleagues hurried over
with all kinds of presents. Dapei arrived too, carrying a
basket of flowers. Afterward, Mei saw Dapei to the door,

and he appeared to be making a promise to her, patting his palm on his chest in the gathering dusk.

At the lane entrance, we stopped Dapei, who still recognized some of us. The following was what he told us:

"Last month, our factory finally had a chance to win a multimillion yuan contract, from an entrepreneur named Huang Weizhong. A lot of companies were competing for the contract. We don't have much of an advantage over our rivals. The usual PR efforts wouldn't have had an effect on him, since he knows the market like the back of his hand. He declared that he was fed up with those karaoke girls and Japanese massages, and it would be an insult to approach him like that. Nevertheless, he had a weak point, or in his own words, a strong point. He saw himself as unmatched at the dining table—so far unrivaled, swallowing like a wolf, devouring like a tiger. That's how he had got his nickname—Tiger Huang. So he had proposed a condition to his business associates as a sort of a joke: whoever could outdo him drinking and eating at a banquet would get the order. But I didn't take it as a joke. The contract was crucial for the survival of our factory—it was a battle we could not afford to lose. So everyone looked to Wei.

"The special banquet of twenty-four courses arranged by Wei was called the Complete Manchurian and Han. The name must have originated in the Qing dynasty, as the Manchurian emperor, eager to show his supreme rule over China, brought in delicacies from the different ethnic groups all over the land and served them on one palace dinner table. Camel dome, bear paw, swallow nest, monkey brains . . . all the rarities imaginable under the sun. Wei also arranged for a bevy of singing girls, dressed in transparent gauze with cloudlike trails, dancing barefoot to ancient music, as if soaring miraculously out of the Dunhuang murals, as was supposed to be common at the palace.

"Tiger Huang came to the banquet and proved himself worthy of his nickname. He fell to with the fierceness of a tiger, but Wei showed no less ferocity. The camel domes, which looked like pure fat, disappeared under their chopsticks in two or three minutes. So did the bear paws stewed in rich gravy. Then the live monkey was brought to the table with its scalp shaved, staring up at the two gourmands with terror in its eyes. Without a blink, Huang signaled the waiter to go ahead with the task of crushing the monkey skull, and spooned out the white and red brain onto Wei's platter before he swallowed a mouthful. They finished three bottles of liquor before half of the courses were served. Huang started *huaquan*, flourishing his hand and shouting like mad. Wei smelled blood, throwing off his jacket and hacking at the table with the edge of his palm like an ax. It was appalling to witness the battle raging between the two, as if they had an irreconcilable hatred against each other.

"Others started slipping out of the banquet room in consternation. Huang and Wei dominated the scene with an oppressive, violent *qi*. Those dancing girls were ordered to leave too. Huang had finally met his match, he proclaimed, and there was no need for the cheap stimulation. Transfixed, we stayed outside and looked in through the glass with bated breath. All of a sudden, Huang did something totally incomprehensible to us outside, for we couldn't hear what they were saying. Holding the cup, he had his arm crossed with Wei's. It was an intimate gesture, usually between man and woman in love, like a sign of a pledge. Then Huang started wiping his nose and eyes vigorously, gulping straight from a bottle of Maotai, as if there were no tomorrow. So did Wei.

"We waited outside for more than three hours. Finally, Wei helped Huang stagger out of the banquet room. Huang kept calling Wei 'Elder Brother,' with his arm on Wei's shoulder. Huang still had enough wit about him to summon his secretary and, mumbling about the contract, the deal was sealed.

"Later that night, Wei was rushed to the hospital, his stomach hurting as if being pierced by a thousand knives.

"The second morning, while Wei was still in the hospital, another company contacted Huang, suggesting that Huang was the winner at the banquet because he had come out unscratched. In other words, he did not have to give the order to us. Huang said, shaking his head, 'Wei risked his life keeping me company at the banquet. The least I can do is to keep my word.'

"So how can we not be grateful to Wei?" Dapei concluded. "We want him to take a good rest. After he has recovered, there will be a lot of work for him in our factory."

Sure enough, Tiger Huang kept his promise by sending the signed contract to the factory. He also sent to Red Dust Lane a bulging red envelope, the thickness of which—according to Four-Eyed Liu who saw Mei taking it from a carrier—suggested that a generous amount was enclosed.

"It's a changed world," Four-Eyed Liu commented. "A wine sack and rice bag can be of some use too!"

"Do you think he can eat and drink as before?" Old Root raised a rhetorical question.

The doctor had given Wei a serious warning, as we heard, about his way of eating and drinking. If he didn't mend his ways, there would be nothing the doctor could do to help the next time Wei was sent to the hospital.

"But what else could Wei possibly do," Old Root followed with another rhetorical question, "if he did not eat and drink as before?"

Lottery

(2005)

This is the last issue of *Red Dust Lane Blackboard Newsletter* for the year 2005. Another year full of victories for our great country. The airplanes chartered for the Chinese Lunar New Year holiday made the first flights between China and Taiwan since 1949. China and Russia held their first joint military exercises. In October, China conducted its second manned space flight, with two astronauts circling the earth in the Shenzhou capsule. We're aware of the problems and challenges in the new era, of course. The explosion of the petrochemical plant in the Jilin province caused major pollution of the Songhua River, an incident that brought attention to the environmental issues in China, and our government took effective measures. This year, China's GDP grew by 9.9 percent.

In Red Dust Lane, quite a lot of things were taken for granted. Especially prone to doing so was Auntie Jia, the celebrated matchmaker of the lane, as she calculated the feasibility of two young people as a couple. That was how she had seen and determined Jin and Qing to be a possible couple years earlier.

Jin had an iron bowl of a job in a state-run factory. He was a good, honest man, but weak, diffident almost to a fault. Qing, an ex–educated youth and a single mother, though allegedly a knockout in her days, worked at an eel booth in the neighborhood food market and had a small room in the lane. They were both in their thirties. So on Auntie Jia's matchmaking scale, they were almost equal.

"What makes a couple happy?" Auntie Jia answered her own question. "Not beauty. Not money. But balance. Once the scale tips, trouble comes."

Based on such a realistic calculation, Jin and Qing were married. Neither of them was perfect, so each wouldn't expect too much of the other. As Auntie Jia had predicted, they got along quite well. On summer evenings, people could see Qing chopsticking a piece of pork into Jin's bowl, and his waving the rattan fan for her. Her son from a previous marriage in the countryside took to Jin too. Ordinary, but just like most people in the lane, they were supposed to live their lives ordinarily ever after.

But nothing can be taken for granted in this world. In China's economic reform, Jin's state-run factory lost steam, and his pay suffered a drastic cut. He didn't see himself be-

ing in a position to protest, but it was an increasingly unbearable fact that he earned less than his eel-preparing
wife.

Hers was not an easy job, for the rice paddy eels had
to be prepared alive—it made a world of difference in taste.
Shanghai housewives would never buy the eels already
prepared by the peddlers. So starting in the early morning,
Qing stood at the booth near the back exit of the lane, preparing the slippery and struggling eels for the customers
who demanded that the process be completed before their
eyes. For her service, they paid little and sometimes nothing. It was conventional, however, that they leave the bones
and offal for her. She made her money by selling the bones
to a restaurant known for its special eel bone soup noodles or to her cat-keeping neighbors, who would cook eel-
flavored rice as an occasional treat for their rat-catching
cats. She was a capable wife, using whatever was left over
for meals at home, making a delicious soup, creamy with
a handful of chopped green onions, that was supposedly
quite nutritious too.

According to a proverb, when the roof leaks, it rains all
night. At the same time Jin had his salary cut at his factory,
Qing's eel-preparing business also started going downhill. The noodle restaurant lost customers due to a rumor
about the eels being fed hormones. And for some mysterious reason, the number of rats also decreased in the
neighborhood, while some young people spoke out against
feeding cats fish or eel bones, claiming it was a sort of pet

abuse. She had no choice but to work harder and longer at the half-deserted booth, sometimes until seven or eight in the evening.

Eventually, she turned into an inveterately nagging wife, complaining in the lane about her "incapable husband." But for his incompetence, she wouldn't have to toil and moil like that, her hands covered in eel blood all day long.

There was something to her argument, Jin admitted to himself. He felt guilty at the sight of her collapsing when back home, unwashed, after slaving for more than twelve hours at the eel booth. How could he ever talk back? He was worried sick, growing even thinner. In the summer evening, he sat out alone, stripped to his waist, his emaciated chest looking like a wooden washboard, worn out by all the dirty laundry of the time. After all, however delicious the eel bone soup might have been, no one could live on it alone.

What made things worse for the couple in the lane was the fact that things got better for a number of their neighbors. In China's reform, a lot of people enjoyed tremendous material improvement. The sharp contrast between them and their neighbors fueled Qing's indignant frustration.

"With a pathetic man like you, what can I expect?"

In desperation, Jin started buying lottery tickets, at first in secret, with the money he got from occasional carpentry jobs after his factory work. He saved every penny from these jobs for the lottery, but since he gave her all his factory salary, she never suspected that he was doing anything behind her back. But other people in the lane bought lottery too, and eventually someone mentioned it to her.

"He's penniless, and luckless too," she said, sitting outside, shaking her head, and resting her eel-blood-covered bare feet on a bamboo stool. She hadn't washed yet after a long day's work because inside the single tiny room, her son was doing his homework, with which Jin was supposed to help. "Like a tombstone-crushed turtle, it can never turn."

One evening, Qing was sitting outside like that, waiting for her turn to wash after her son finished his homework, when Jin rushed out, wearing only one plastic slipper, shouting, "Lottery! I have won the lottery. The jackpot."

"What?" She looked up, her hand clutching the back of the bamboo chair like a wriggling eel. "You're joking!"

But he did not appear to be. In fact, he hadn't joked with her for years. There was something different in his voice. A light flashed out of his eyes as he set off in a trot toward the lane entrance, waving a torn page of the newspaper in his hand.

"The jackpot," he repeated, his mouth covered in white foam like a stranded crab in the food market.

Before she could react, he was out of sight. The neighbors gathered around. Some of them had heard about him buying a lottery ticket the week before. No one could be sure, however, that he had really won the lottery. To be sure, they had to see the lottery ticket, and whether he had it with him or where he kept it, Qing had no idea.

To the neighbors' surprise, Jin returned from the back entrance of the lane, as if the lane made up the entire world of his existence.

There was no lottery ticket in his hand, only that torn newspaper, which Four-Eyed Liu snatched from him. Stripped to his waist, Jin had on only a pair of short pants with no pockets—he clearly did not have the ticket on his person. He kept running, without pausing, heading to the front entrance again. No one could stop him: he seemed not to hear or see anyone.

Searching through the room, sure she had looked in every possible place, Qing finally unearthed a notebook that contained the numbers of the lottery tickets he had bought. Auntie Jia also came over, bringing the newspaper with the number of the winning lottery printed in red. One of the numbers matched, and the prize was a million yuan.

But the ticket itself was nowhere. "What an ill-starred woman I am," Qing wailed heartbrokenly. "Finally, we hit the jackpot, but my husband has lost the ticket, and his mind too."

More and more people gathered around. Some of them had come for the evening talk of the lane and witnessed the unexpected drama.

Jin was running back a second time, still waving his hand, as if grasping the lottery ticket.

"What now, Old Root?" one of the neighbors asked.

"Well," Old Root said, squinting his eyes slightly in the cigarette smoke. "Who is he most afraid of?"

"His wife, the so-called roaring tiger east of the river."

"Bring her over."

Qing came running. Old Root, a legendary figure in the lane, was known for giving wise advice.

"Slap his face hard," he said. "Tell him at the highest pitch of your voice that it's been nothing but a spring and autumn dream, and that he has won no lottery."

"But how can I? He is a millionaire now. If he learns that I have slapped him, he will never forgive me."

"Have you never done so before?"

"Well, but that's different. Now he could throw me away like the eel bone at the bottom of the soup pot."

"Don't worry about such things. Do it, woman."

So when Jin ran back yet another time, she steeled herself to go over and slap his face as hard as she could.

"You're dreaming about the lottery, you idiot."

He was stunned into standing still, staring at her in horror, his ghastly pale face streaked with the eel blood from her hand, before he suddenly reeled and slumped to the ground.

"Oh now what are we going to do—" she wailed, stamping her bare feet on the dust of the lane.

But Jin was coming to. Still staggering, he struggled up with his hand on the lane wall. The frantic light in his eyes gone, he stammered, henpecked, as always.

"Oh, I'm so-so-sorry, wife. I should have told you earlier. I bought lo-lo-lottery tickets in secret."

"No, I'm sorry—for everything, husband—"

"Where's the ticket?" Old Root cut in. "Give it to her!"

"Yes, it's in the toolbox inside," he said obediently. "I'll go get it."

But Qing didn't follow him into the room. Instead, she stood in the lane, holding her one hand in the other as if in great pain.

"What's the problem?"

"My hand can hardly move. People say a lottery winner must be predestined from high above—like a star—and I actually slapped his face like that. My hand is paralyzed as punishment, I'm afraid."

"Don't be ridiculous. Your slap has saved your man."

"How?" a young boy in the crowd asked out of curiosity. "A slap!"

"The excitement of winning the lottery was too much, driving him over the edge. He needed a blow—a blow on the head, as in a Zen story, to shock him back to reality," Old Root said, shaking his head. "Who scares him the most?"

"That makes sense. Don't worry about it, Qing. That's a slap of endearment," Four-Eyed Liu observed.

But she was already running into the room, her arms swinging.

"It's probably because of the eel blood," Auntie Jia commented, as if in unexpected enlightenment. "Jin was possessed by an evil spirit. What's the most effective antidote to evil spirits? Animal blood, as you must have read in many classical Chinese novels."

"That must be a nutritious slap too," another neighbor said, "leaving enough eel blood on his face to make a bowl of soup."

"No, I'm not going to make any eel bone soup," Qing said, coming out with a smile bursting out of her tears, holding a small piece of paper in her hand. "I don't have to—with such a husband, with the lottery ticket."

10/2010